THE
ROMANTIC
EGOISTS

THE

ROMANTIC

EGOISTS

Louis Auchincloss

GREENWOOD PRESS, PUBLISHERS
WESTPORT, CONNECTICUT

To Jim and Anne Thomas
and to my godson, Jimmie

Certains hommes éloignent d'eux le tragique. Dans le petit et dans le grand. Cela va de l'écrasé dans la rue, qu'ils ne sont jamais là pour voir, aux bombes et aux mitraillades qui les entourent de toutes parts sans les toucher. Ils ne sont pas plus timorés que d'autres, et ne se mettent pas plus à l'abri. Au contraire, leur imagination peut avoir le goût et quelque désir de l'épreuve tragique. Rien à faire: le drame ne frappe pas où ils sont. Ils traversent la guerre et les révolutions sans avoir vu une seule fois un cadavre, sans savoir comment cela est fait. Incurablement préservés, et bourgeois malgré eux.

HENRI DE MONTHERLANT

CONTENTS

BILLY AND
THE GARGOYLES

BILLY AND THE GARGOYLES

SHIRLEY SCHOOL IN APPEARANCE WAS GLOOMY ENOUGH to look at, but it was only when we returned there in later years that it seemed so to us. As boys, we took its looks for granted. The buildings were grouped in orderly lines around a square campus; they were of gray stone and had tall, Gothic windows. The ceilings inside were high, making large wall spaces which were covered with faded lithographs of Renaissance paintings. There was a chapel, a gymnasium, a schoolhouse, several dormitories and, scattered about at a little distance from the campus, the cottages of the married masters. No fence separated the school from the surrounding New England countryside, but none was needed. Shirley was a community unto itself; its very atmosphere prohibited escape or intrusion. The runaway boy would know that he was only running from his own future, and a trespasser would immediately feel that he was intruding on futures never intended for him. For Shirley, even through the shabby stone of its lamentable architecture, exuded the atmosphere of a hundred years of accumulated idealism. You were made as a boy to feel that great things would be expected of you after graduation; you would rise in steady ascent on the escalator of success as inevitably as you rose from one form to another in the school. Life was a pyramid, except that there was more room at the top, and anyone who had been through the dark years of hazing and athletic competitions, who had prayed and washed and conformed at Shirley, should and would get there. It was good to be ambitious because, being educated and God-fearing, you would raise the general level as you yourself rose to power, to riches, to a bishopric or to the presidency of a large university. At the end there was death, it was true, but with it even greater rewards, and old age, unlike Macbeth's, would be sweetened by a respectful lull broken only by the rattle of applause at testimonial dinners. I find that I can still look at life and feel that it ought to be this way, that I can still vaguely wonder why one year has not put me farther ahead than its predecessor. There were no such doubts at Shirley, unless they were felt by Billy Prentiss.

Billy was my cousin and the only other boy at school whom I knew when I went there first at the age of thirteen. The contrast between us, however, was not one to make me presume on the relationship. Billy came of a large and prosperous family, and I was an only child whose mother gave bridge lessons at summer hotels to help with my Shirley tuition. Billy, though thin and far from strong, was tall and fair and had an easygoing, outgiving personality; I was short, dark and of a truculent disposition. But these contrasts were as nothing before the overriding distinction between the "old kid" and the "new kid." Billy and I may have been in the same form, but he had completed a year at the school before my arrival, which gave him great social prerogatives. By Shirley's rigid code there should have been only the most formal relations between us.

Billy, however, did not recognize the code. That is what I mean when I say that he had doubts at Shirley. He greeted me from the first in a friendly manner that was entirely improper, as if we had been at home and not at school. He helped me to unpack and showed me my gymnasium locker and supplied me with white stiff collars for Sunday wear. He talked in an easy, chatty manner about how my mother had taught him bridge and what he had seen during the summer with his family in Europe, as if he believed that such things could be balanced against the things that were happening at Shirley, the real things. He was certainly an odd figure for an old kid; I think of him now as he looked during my first months at school, stalking through the corridors of the Lower Forms Building on his way to or from the library, running the long fingers of his left hand through his blond hair and whistling "Mean To Me." He lived in a world of his own, and, with all my gratitude, I was sufficiently conservative to wonder if it wasn't Utopian. It embarrassed me, for example, when he was openly nice to me in the presence of other old kids.

"How are you getting on, Peter?" he asked me one morning after chapel as we walked to the schoolhouse. Nobody else called me by my Christian name. "Have you got everything you need? Can I lend you any books or clothes?"

"No, I'm fine, thank you."

"You're a cousin, you know," he said, looking at me seriously. "Cousins ought to help each other out. Even second cousins."

I didn't really believe that anyone could help me. Homesickness was like cutting teeth or having one's tonsils out. I nodded, but said nothing.

"If you have any trouble with the old kids, let me know," he continued. "I could speak to them. It might help."

"Oh, no please!" I explained. Nothing could have more impressed me with his otherworldliness than a suggestion so unorthodox. "You mustn't do that! It wouldn't be the thing at all!"

We were interrupted by voices from behind us, loud, sneering voices. It was what I had been afraid of.

"Is that Prentiss I see talking to a new kid? Can he so demean himself?"

"Do you pal around with new kids, Billy?"

"What's come over you, Prentiss?"

The last voice was stern; it was George Neale's.

"Peter Westcott happens to be my cousin," Billy answered with dignity, turning around to face them. "And there's nothing in the world wrong with him. Is there a law that I may not talk to my own cousin?"

He turned again to me, but I hurried ahead to join a group of new kids. I'm afraid I was shocked that he should speak in this fashion to a boy like George Neale. George, after all, was one of the undisputed leaders of the form. He was a small, fat, clumsy boy who commanded by the sheer deadliness of his tongue and the intensity of his animosities. He also enjoyed an immunity from physical retaliation through the reputation of a bad heart, the after-effect, it was generally said, of a childhood attack of rheumatic fever. He had chosen for his mission in school the persecution of those who failed to meet exactly the rigid standards of social behavior that our formmates, represented by himself, laid down. I sometimes wonder, in trying to recollect how George first appeared to me, if he derived the fierce satisfaction from his activities that I believed at the time. It seems more probable, as I bring back the straight, rather rigid features of his round face and his tone of dry impatience, that he looked at nonconformists as Spanish Inquisitors looked at heretics who were brought before them, as part of the day's work, something that had to be done, boring and arduous though it might be. Why George should have been chosen as the avenging agent of the gods it was not for him to ask; what mattered only was that they required, for dim but cogent reasons of their own, a division of the world into the oppressed and their oppressors. He and his victims were the instruments of these gods, caught in the ruthless pattern of what was and what was not "Shirley," a pattern more fundamental and significant in the lives of all of us than the weak and distant humanitarianism of the faculty, who brooded above us, benevolent but powerless to help, like the twentieth-century protestant God whom we worshiped in the Gothic chapel.

George was in charge of the program of hazing the new kids, and Billy's ill-considered kindness only resulted in bringing me prematurely to his attention. Custom required that each new kid be singled out for a particular ordeal, and I was soon made aware, from the conversation of the old kids who raised their voices as I passed, that mine had been decided on. Apparently I was to have my head shaved. I lived from this point on in such an agony of apprehension that it was almost a relief to discover one Sunday morning, from the atmosphere of huddles and whispers around me, that George had chosen his moment. I retreated instinctively to the library to stay there until chapel, but the first time I looked up from the book I was pretending to read, it was to find George and the others gathered before me.

"Won't you come outside, Westcott?" George asked me in a mild, dry tone. "We'd like to have a little talk with you."

"It won't take a minute, Westcott," another added with a leer.

No violence was allowed in the library; it was sanctuary. I could have waited until the bell for chapel and departed in safety. George knew this, but he knew too, as I knew, and he knew that I knew it, that the fruition of his scheme was like the fall of Hamlet's sparrow: if it was not now, it would be still to come. I got up without a word and walked out of the library, down the corridor and out to the back lawn. There I turned around and faced them.

There was a moment of hesitation, and then someone pushed me. I went sprawling over on the grass, for George, unnoticed, had knelt behind me. They all jumped on me, and I struggled violently, too violently, destroying whatever sympathy might have been latent in them by giving one boy, whose heart was not really in it, a vicious kick in the stomach. In another moment I was overwhelmed and held firmly down while George produced the razor. I closed my eyes and felt giddy with hatred.

Then the miracle occurred. I distinctly heard a window open and a voice cry:

"Cheese it, fellows! Mr. O'Neil!"

And in a second twenty hands had released me, and I heard the thump of retreating feet in the earth under my head. I sat up dazedly and looked around. Nobody was there but Billy; he was standing inside the building looking out at me through an open window. He smiled and climbed over the low sill. He was actually helping me to my feet.

"Where did they go?" I demanded.

"They beat it."

"But why?"

He laughed.

"Didn't you hear me?"

I stared at him in perplexity.

"Then where's Mr. O'Neil?" I asked.

He laughed again.

"How should I know?"

I rubbed my head.

"Why did you do it, Billy?" I asked.

He helped me brush the grass off my blue suit.

"Because you're my cousin," he said cheerfully. "And because they're down on you. Isn't that enough?"

I felt for the first time since I had come to Shirley that I might be going to cry.

"They'll be back," I pointed out, "when they find out."

"Then let's clear out."

"You go," I said. "They're not after you."

Incredibly, he laughed again.

"They will be now."

Again we heard the stamping of feet, this time from within the building. The door burst open, and they surrounded us.

"What's the idea, Prentiss?" George snarled, stepping out of the circle toward him. "Where's Mr. O'Neil?"

Billy shrugged his shoulders and put his hands in his pockets.

"Didn't you see him? He and his wife were coming over by the hedge on their way to chapel."

He flung this off coolly, as if to him it was a matter of the utmost indifference whether or not he was believed. Then he gave his attitude a further emphasis by turning to me, quite casually, and smiling.

"We saw them, didn't we, Peter?" he said.

"Well, *we* didn't!" George cried.

"I can't be bothered with what you see and don't see," Billy retorted. "If you didn't, you didn't."

"Are you siding with Westcott, Prentiss?" George demanded. "Are you on the side of the new kids? Is that where you stand, Prentiss?"

He glanced from side to side at the others as he said this. "What about it, Billy?"

"Are you with the new kids, Billy?"

"Let's *get* Prentiss!"

But just then the bell for assembly, at long last, jangled sharply from within the building, and the crowd burst

apart and rushed up the steps to the door. I can still remember the fierce joy with which, as George Neale leaned
down to pick up the comb that had slipped from his pocket,
I stamped on it and broke it in two. He didn't even bother
to look at me, but turned and hurried after his friends.

George was not a boy to let an assembly bell stand between
him and his victim, and I lived for days in dread of a re-
newed effort to execute the head-shaving plan. I soon
found out, however, that I had nothing personally to be
afraid of. George, it was rumored, had put the new kids
quite out of his mind; he was concentrating his energies on
a project against the person whose basic challenge of authority he had so immediately recognized. One Sunday
after chapel, when Billy was waylaid by the gang and pelted
with the icy snowballs of the season's first snow, his books
flung in the mud and the lining ripped from his hat, we
knew that George's campaign had begun in earnest.

"I don't know if I'm quite as popular as I supposed,"
Billy told me, with a sort of desperate gaiety, as he and I
engaged in the sorry task of collecting his books and rubbing them off. "I would suggest that I might be a good
person to stay away from for a while."

"Cousins should help each other," I said tersely. "You
told me that."

Every persecution has a pattern, and George soon revealed the nature of his. It was to establish that Billy was
really not a boy at all, not even an effeminate boy, but a
girl. This was carried out with the special vindictiveness
which old kids reserved for other old kids who had been

disloyal. George devised not one but several nicknames for his victim; Billy became known as "Bella," then as "Angela" and finally, with a venomous simplicity, as "Woman." George trained his boys to carry through the identification with a completeness that would have done credit to a secret police. He knew at an early age that the way to break a human being is never to relax, to follow him through the day and into the night until he lets down his guard for just a moment, a private moment, alone in his cubicle, in the lavatory, in his seat at chapel, and then to strike hardest. If George and the others found Billy taking a shower in the morning when they came into the lavatory, they would act like men who have stumbled into a ladies' room. "Eek!" they would shriek. "It's Angela! Excuse me." And they would leave the lavatory and insist on waiting outside even when the prefect on duty came by and ordered them in to take their showers, shouting in voices clearly audible to poor Billy: "But we can't go in! There's a naked woman in there," until the bewildered prefect would go in and find Billy and order them in, but not without a leer to show that he sided with the conspirators, grinning at their joke and looking the other way when, upon entering, they pelted Billy with pieces of soap, crying, "Cover her up! For the sake of decency cover her up!" George was careful to carry the use of the female pronoun into every department of life at school; if commenting on a translation of Billy's in Latin class he would say, even if reprimanded, "She left off the adjective in line ten, sir," or filing into the schoolroom for prayers he would always step aside, pushing the others with him, on Billy's arrival and cry,

"Ladies first!" Even in chapel, the sacred chapel, where the headmaster, lost in illusion, believed that freedom of worship existed, I have seen Billy, intensely religious as one can only be at thirteen, interrupted from his devotions by having a hat jammed on his head by George, crouching in the pew ahead, and hearing him hiss: "Ladies always wear hats in church. Didn't Saint Paul say so?"

Billy's reaction to all of this seemed designed to bring out the worst in George. He simply appeared to ignore the whole thing. He would stare blankly, at times even pityingly at the crowd that baited him and then turn on his heel, carefully smoothing back the hair which they would inevitably have rumpled. He never seemed to lose his temper or strike back except when he was physically overwhelmed and pinned to the ground and then in a sudden galvanization of wheeling arms and legs, with closed eyes, he would try to fight himself free with an ineffective frenzy that only aroused laughter. But such moments were rare. For the most part he was remote and disdainful, like a marquise in a tumbrel looking over the heads of the mob.

The very fact that I think of a marquise and not a marquis shows the effectiveness of George's propaganda. I saw it all, for I stayed close to Billy throughout this period. The fact that he was in trouble on my account overcame, I am glad to say, my instinctive, if rather sullen, deference to the majority. And then, too, I should add, there was a certain masochistic pleasure in sacrificing myself on the altar of Billy's unpopularity. My real difficulty came less in sharing his distress than in sharing his attitude of superiority to it, for I believed, superstitiously, in all the things that he sneered at. I believed, as George believed, in the system, the hazing, in the whole grim division of the school world into those who "belonged" and those who didn't. The fact that I was one of the latter, partly at my own election, was not important; I was still a part of the system. It bothered me that Billy, on our Sunday walks in the country, insisted on discussing faraway, unreal things — home and his mother and her friends and what they did and talked about. He would never talk about George Neale, for example. One afternoon I made a point of this.

"Do you suppose there will always be people like Neale in life?" I asked him as we walked down the wooded path to the river. "Will we always have to be watching out for them?"

"George?" Billy queried, as if not quite sure to whom I had referred. He paused. "Why, people like George simply don't exist in my parents' world." He shrugged his shoulders. "After all, you can't spend your time throwing snowballs at people and expect to be invited out much. You don't make friends by going up to your host at a party and calling him by a woman's name."

"But he might learn to do other things, mightn't he?" I persisted. "Spread lies and things like that?"

"My dear Peter," Billy said with an amiable condescension, "George will be utterly helpless without his gang. And his gang, you see, will have grown up."

But he couldn't quite dispel my idea that some of the ugliness that was George might survive the grim barriers of our school days. Billy's faith in the future was a touching faith in a warm and sunny world where people moved

to and fro without striking each other and conversed without insults, a world where the idea was appreciated, the
mannerism ignored. I could feel the attraction of this
future, so different from the Shirley future of struggle and
success; I could even yearn for it, but try as I would, I could
never quite bring myself to believe in it. As the sky grew
darker and we turned back to the school and saw ahead
over the trees the Gothic tower of the chapel, my heart
contracted with a sense of guilt that I had been avoiding,
even for an afternoon, the sober duty of facing Shirley facts.

"I don't know if the world will be so terribly different
from school," I said gloomily. "I bet it's very much the
same."

Even Billy's face clouded at this. It was as if I had voiced
a doubt that he was desperately repressing, a doubt that
if admitted would have made his troubles at school too
much to bear. He gazed up at the tower, anticipating perhaps all that we were returning to, the changing of shirts
and collars, the evening meal, the long study period amid
the sniggering, the note-passing, the sly kick from the desk
behind.

"It should have gargoyles, like cathedrals in Europe," he
said suddenly. "Grinning little gargoyles like George
Neale."

Even George could not keep a thing going forever, and
the persecution of Billy at length became a bore to his gang.
We had been through the long New England winter, and
in the spring of second-form year we were beginning to
emerge as individuals from the gray anonymity of child-

hood. We were even forming friendships based on something besides mutual insecurity and joint hostility to
others, friendships more intense than any relationships that
we were to know for many years. It was a time in our lives
that the headmaster viewed with suspicion, conducive, as
he believed it to be, to a state of mind which he darkly
described as "sentimental," but it was nonetheless exciting
to us to be aware of ourselves for the first time as something other than boys at Shirley. We were beginning to
discover, in spite of everything, that there were not only
blacks and whites, but reds and yellows in the world around
us and that life itself could be something more than a struggle.

It seems clear to me now that George must have resented
our maturing and the breakup of the old hard line between the accepted and the unaccepted. He tried to maintain his waning control over his group by reminding boys
of their ungainliness and ineptitudes of a few months before, by reviving old issues and screaming the battle cries
that used to range the group against the individual. He
sought new victims, new scapegoats, but public opinion was
increasingly unmanageable. George represented the past,
or at most the passing; he was like an angry Indian medi-
cine man who finds his tribe turning away to the attractions
of a broader civilization. Though he could beat his drum
and dance his dance, though he could even still manage to
burn a few victims, essentially his day was over. But if
George had been left behind, so, oddly enough, had Billy.
Instead of stepping forward to take his place among the
boys who would now have received him, he preferred to

remain alone and aloof. He seemed tired, now that the ordeal was over, discouraged, just when there was hope. It was as if, in the struggle, he had received a small, deep wound that was only now beginning to fester. George, deprived of other victims, seemed to sense this, for he pressed the attack against Billy all alone, with a desperate vindictiveness, as if to deliver the last and fatal blow of which his declining power was capable. Their conflict had come to be an individual thing, almost a curiosity to the rest of us. They stood apart, fighting their own fight, quaint if rather grim reminders of a standard of values that had passed.

Toward the middle of spring Billy developed the habit of reporting sick to the infirmary. He would go there for two or three days at a time, using the old trick of touching his thermometer to a lamp bulb when the nurse was out of the room. The infirmary had its pleasant side; like the library it was sanctuary, an insulated white box where one could stay in bed and read the thick, rebound volumes of Dickens and Baroness Orczy. It so happened that we were both there, I with a sinus infection and he with the pretense of one, on the day of the game with Pollock School, the great event of the baseball season. I hated to miss the game, for it involved a half holiday, a trip to Pollock and a celebration afterward if we won. Billy, less regretful, was sharing a room with me on the empty second floor.

Late in the afternoon of the game, as we were working on a picture puzzle, Mrs. Jones, the matron's assistant, hurried in, greatly excited. One of the masters had just telephoned from Pollock to report that we had won the game. I gave a little yell of enthusiasm, partly sincere, partly perfunctory. Billy looked at me bleakly.

"Now we'll have that damn celebration," he said curtly. "Drums and cheers, drums and cheers, all night. God! And for what?"

He lost all interest in what we were doing and refused to discuss it with me. He lay back in bed and simply stared at the ceiling while I turned back to the unfinished puzzle.

It was late in the afternoon, about six o'clock, when the buses which had taken the school to Pollock began to return. We could hear the crunch of their wheels on the drive on the other side of the building and the excited yells of the disembarking boys. From across the campus came the muffled roll of the drums. Already the celebration was starting. The entire school and all the masters would now assemble before the steps of the headmaster's house. He would come out in a straw hat and a red blazer and be raised to the shoulders of the school prefect on a chair strapped to two poles. Waving his megaphone he would be borne away at the head of a procession to a martial tune of the fife and drum corps on a circuit of all the school buildings. Before each of these the crowd would stop and in response to the headmaster's deep "What have we here?" would shout the name of the building followed by the school cheer. As the slow procession wended its way around the campus it would become noisier and the cheers more numerous; wives of popular masters would be thunderously applauded and would have to appear at the windows of their houses to acknowledge the ovation; statues, gates, memorial fountains would be cheered until the procession wound up by the athletic field, where a bonfire would be built and the members of the triumphant team tossed aloft by multitudinous arms and cheered in the flickering light of the flames. And all the while the "outside," the big bell over the gymnasium which sounded the hours for rising, for going to chapel, for attending meals, a knell that brought daily to the countryside the austere routine of Shirley School, would toll and toll, symbolizing in its shocking unrestraint the extraordinary liberty of the day.

The atmosphere pervaded even the infirmary. Mrs. Gardner, the matron, and her assistant watched from the dispensary window. The infirmary cook gave Billy and me an extra helping of ice cream. I moved my bed over to the window and listened to the distant throb of the band. When it stopped we would know that the headmaster was speaking and a moment later would come the roar of the school cheer. Glancing at Billy, after one of these roars, I noticed that he looked pale and tense.

"Listen to that damn bell," he complained, when he saw me looking at him. "It gets on my nerves. It's like Saint Bartholomew's Day, with everyone coming after the Huguenots."

I said nothing to this, but there was something contagious about his tensity. As the shouts grew louder and more distinct, as we finally made out the stamp of feet, I got out of my bed and pushed it away from the window.

"What are you doing?" Billy asked me sharply. "Are you ashamed of being in the infirmary?"

He sat up suddenly and got out of bed. He walked to the open window and stood before it, his hands on his hips. From behind him, looking into the courtyard below, I could see the first boys arriving, waving school banners and blowing horns.

"Billy, get back," I begged him. "They'll see you! Please, Billy!"

Then I spotted the headmaster's chair coming around the corner of the adjacent building and ducked out of sight. Billy ignored me completely. From below, through the open windows, almost unbelievably close now, came the din of the assembling school. The drums kept beating, and laughter and jokes, often from recognizable voices, came to our ears. It seemed to me, as I shrank against the wall near the window, pressing my spinal cord against its white coldness, as though every shout and drumbeat, every retort, detaching itself from the general roar and suddenly coherent, every laugh and cheer, each sound of feet on gravel, was part of some huge reptilian figure surrounding the infirmary and our very room with the cold, muscular coils of its body. Fear pounded in me, sharp and irrational.

"Billy!" I called again at him. "Billy!"

There was a sudden silence outside, and we heard the rich, assured tones of the headmaster's voice, starting his classic interrogatory to the crowd.

"What is this building that I see before me?"

"The infirmary!" thundered the school.

"And who is the good lady who runs the infirmary?"

"Mrs. Gardner!"

"And does Mrs. Gardner have an assistant?"

"Mrs. Jones," roared the crowd.

This would have been followed immediately, in normal procedure, by the headmaster's request for cheers for the infirmary and for the good women who ran it. Instead there was an unexpected pause, a silence, and then, as my blood froze I heard the headmaster's other voice, his disciplinary voice, directed up and into the very window at which Billy was standing.

"Who is that boy in the window? Go away from that window, boy, and get to bed." It then added, with a chuckle for the benefit of the crowd: "Good gracious me, anyone might think he wasn't sick." There was a roar of laughter.

Billy, however, continued to stand there as if he hadn't heard, and the momentary hush that followed was broken by the sharp, clear tones of George Neale.

"Go back to bed, Angela! Can't you hear? Take the wax out of your ears!"

Once again there was a startled quiet. The amazement must have been as much at George's impudence as at Billy's immobility; it was unheard of for a boy to second the headmaster's order. The old struggle between George and Billy hung like a lantern in the darkening air before the upturned eyes of three hundred boys. It may have been the use of his nickname, the bold, casual, unconventional use of it before the boys and the faculty, before Mrs. Gardner and Mrs. Jones watching from the window of the dispensary, before the townspeople from Shirley who had come to watch the celebration, that broke Billy down. It was as if he had been stamped "Angela" unredeemably and for the ages. The future, in spite of all his protest, would be a Shirley future. He suddenly waved his arms in a frenzied, circular fashion at the mob.

"Three cheers for Pollock!" he screamed in a harsh voice that did not sound like him at all. "Three cheers for Pollock School!" he screamed. "I wish they'd licked us! I wish they had!"

What I remember feeling at this unbelievable outburst, as I pressed my back harder against the wall, was its inadequacy to express the outrage with which Billy was throbbing. It was too hopelessly disloyal, too hurt, too puerile to do more than dismay or shock. Yet he had said it. He had actually said it! Then the door opened and Mrs. Gardner came in, followed by Mr. O'Neil. I was moved at once to another room, and Billy at last was left alone.

He was taken out of school for good a few days later. His parents drove up from New York and had a long conference with the headmaster. Immediately afterward his things were packed. I was out of the infirmary by then and went to see his mother at the parents' house. She wept a good deal and talked to me as though I were grown up, which flattered me. She said that Billy had had a little "nervous trouble" and would be going home. She added that he was tired and would not be able to see anyone before he left. Then she kissed me and tucked a five-dollar bill in my pocket. I'm afraid that I rather enjoyed my sadness over the whole catastrophe.

At school, after Billy had gone, I did much better. In the ensuing years I rose to be manager of the school press, head librarian and even achieved the dignified status of rober to the headmaster in chapel. Billy diminished in retrospect to a thin, shrill figure lost in the past darkness of lower-school years. But it was only a part of me that felt this way. There was another part that was always uneasy about my disloyalty to the desperate logic of his isolation. It was as though I owed the warmth and friendliness that I later found at Shirley to a compromise that he had not been able to make. Whether or not I was justified in any such reservation can only be determined for himself by each individual who has passed as a boy through that semi-eternity which begins with homesickness and hazing and snowballs and ends, such seeming ages afterwards, with the white flannels and blue coats of commencement in the full glory of a New England spring.

THE FORTUNE OF
ARLEUS KANE

THE FORTUNE OF ARLEUS KANE

LEGEND HAS IT THAT A MAN CAN NEVER SATISFY HIS friends either in the way he spends his money or buries his dead. It always seemed to me, however, that Arleus Kane managed to satisfy his friends at least in the first of these particulars. This, in my opinion, he owed to the fact that he had not simply a lot of money, or even a great deal of it, but a truly enormous quantity. For the spending of the superfortune is judged by special standards, more lenient than those applied to lesser accumulations. Man's natural and perhaps healthy tendency is to be critical of those richer than himself; there is a particular way of life laid down for us by our neighbors to govern our spending in each particular tax bracket right up to the fortune of ten or even fifteen millions. But there or somewhere around there the criticism gradually dies away. We have reached the fresh, clear air of the superfortune, and our neighbors, if there be any left, tend to gather together in silent throngs of wide-eyed Scott Fitzgeralds, barehead before the refracted gleam of our gold.

The heirs of the superfortunes, that is, the conventional ones like Arlie Kane, have much of the same gravity of demeanor that is seen in those royal families that have

managed to hold their thrones through a century and a
half of revolution and social change. Royalty and great
wealth, it might even be said, are on their best behavior in
a day of militant democracy. They seek popular support
by means of a sustained pantomime designed to persuade
the world that they are not what they seem, that they are
not, in other words, really royal or that they are not really
rich. Thus we find the same heavy emphasis on simplicity
of manners, the same careful elimination of eccentricity or
even individuality, the same compulsive habit of making
public utterances about their preference for picnics over
banquets, slacks over evening clothes and whisky or beer
over champagne. Such things repeated often enough come
to be believed; I do not for a minute mean to impugn the
sincerity of the young heirs or princes to whom I refer.
Sincerity, indeed, is apt to be their most striking characteristic. It certainly was so in the case of Arleus Kane.

Arlie was in my form at Shirley School so I have known
him since we were both thirteen. He looked then very
much the way he looks now, large and wide-hipped, with
a clear skin and rumpled blond hair that rose high above
his scalp. His eyes were blue and childishly bright and his
big round chin stuck forward as if he were constantly trying to catch up with something that was getting away from
him. He became almost handsome while we were at
college and law school, but he reverted to the figure of his
boyhood almost immediately thereafter. At Shirley he was
a worried, preoccupied boy who made some of the right
teams and got fairly respectable marks, but only through
the expenditure of what appeared to be an exhausting

effort. Arlie was famous for his violent agonizing before examinations; we were all familiar with the look of desperation in his eyes as he would wail: "Of course you don't have to worry. But I can't remember things. I can't remember *anything.*" As he invariably passed and usually in the first third of the form, he got little enough sympathy, but he would nonetheless go about afterwards asking his bored classmates to congratulate him because "old Lady Luck" had stood by him again. Yes, he was something of a bore, and this kept him from any real popularity in a school where sophistication, at least among the older boys, was at a premium. But Arlie never seemed to mind. He appeared to be perfectly content to consort with the less popular like myself. His private standards, whatever they were, must have kept him too busy to worry about those of others.

We did not at first know anything about the Kane money. As little boys we weren't much interested in such things, and the atmosphere of the school, which had on its roll several names at least as famous as Kane and for the same reason, was perhaps less snobbish than it would have been had they been rarer. As we began to learn, however, from our parents or from those of us who were asked to visit in summer at the Kanes' great place on Long Island, of the magnitude of the fortune that our Arlie would one day inherit, we began to look at him with awe but not with envy, as if he had a curious, grave and somehow rather admirable disease, but nonetheless a disease and not something we would wish for ourselves. We knew it was not Arlie's fault, and we could even sympathize with him, but what we said to each other was the kind of thing we had heard our parents say, such as: "Thank heavens I wasn't born with Arlie's money. Of course, I'd like to be well off, sure, I'd like to have a Lincoln, a place out of town, maybe even a small yacht, but rich like that, good Lord, no!" Even when it occurred to me in secret that it might be rather fun to be rich like that, I tried to repress the thought. Obviously it was a shameful one, and I had no business having it.

It was definitely not the thing to do to tease Arlie about his money. Even during the hazing of our earlier years at school, when the tenderest susceptibilities were considered the fairest game, our family's wealth or poverty, like the personalities of our parents, was out of bounds. There was, however, one boy, Phoenix Weld, who disregarded this unwritten rule. Phoenix was the most sophisticated member of our form; long before the rest of us dared to do anything but stand tongue-tied before girls at sub-scription dances, asking them at the most what school they went to, Phoenix, who scorned such parties as "kid stuff," was sending flowers to chorus girls and telling us, during the bleak, restricted winter months, of the hot spots in Greenwich Village that he would visit on his next vacation. He was a tall, gangling, black-haired, rather dis-agreeable boy who held us in awe with the things which he seemed to know that we didn't know and by his bold and unconventional contempt for the school. As we grew older and began to find his attitude tiresome, he was clever enough to change it. For Phoenix was clever, as clever as he was bitter. I have never known why he was so bitter, but it must have had something to do with his family's ruin in the depression and their attitude toward this catastrophe, for he treated Arlie with a special meanness that rather shocked the rest of us. I remember one day, when he was making a speech on economics in our American history class, he pointed out sneeringly that Theodore Roosevelt had described Arlie's grandfather as a "malefactor of great wealth." Thereafter he always called Arlie, as if it were one word, "malefactorspawn." This would drive poor Arlie, whose good humor usually weathered the rankest abuse, almost to tears, and instead of going to his own defense with his fists as he violently and effectively would on other occasions, he would flush and turn away muttering something about Phoenix being a "stinker." And then the rest of us would all cry: "Leave off that, Phoenix. It's not his fault if he's rich, is it?"

The bitterest conversation between Arlie and Phoenix took place in the winter of our last year at school. The three of us had been asked to lunch on a Sunday by our Latin master and we were crossing the campus after chapel on our way to his house. It was late in the season, and the grass was covered with mud and slush. We wore, of course, our blue suits and stiff collars. Arlie, who had been impressed by a lecture that we had had the night before in vocational guidance, had brought up the subject of what we would do after college.

"I want to go into politics," he said. It was what he had always said. The headmaster, whom Arlie revered inordinately, used to preach sermons to the effect that too few of the school's graduates went into politics, that matters of state were accordingly left to a type of individual known as the professional politician. It was never questioned at Shirley, except by such nonconformists as Phoenix, that such a politician fitted into the social scale somewhere between a pickpocket and a pimp. "Somebody has to do something about taking things out of the hands of the professional politicians."

"Wouldn't you be a professional politician yourself?" Phoenix asked.

Arlie looked blank.

"Certainly not."

"What would you be, then? An amateur?"

"I'd be an independent," Arlie replied blandly. "I'd vote the way I thought was right."

Phoenix shrugged his shoulders and winked at me to indicate the futility of arguing with Arlie. But I didn't wink back. I had no reason to be nice to Phoenix.

"I think I'd rather be a banker," I said, to change the subject. "They're the ones who really control things, aren't they? More than the politicians?"

It was very much the thing, at Shirley, to show signs of exalted ambition.

"You talk as if you were going to boss the world," Phoenix retorted. "Banker, my eye! Politician!" He turned on Arlie. "Who do you think would be desperate enough to vote for you, Kane?"

"What do *you* want to be, Phoenix?" I demanded, before Arlie could answer. "A hat-check boy in one of your night spots?"

"Whatever I am, it'll be more than you are, Westcott,"

he retorted. "That's one thing, at least, you can bank on. Hell, I don't know," he continued, half to himself, as he kicked the snow, "I might be a farmer. If the old man can hang on to his farm till I'm out of college."

I was pleased that Phoenix should show signs of paltry ambition. I visualized a scene in which, hat in hand, he stood before my desk in an office as large as Mussolini's. Oh, he would get his little loan, of course, but not by check. He would get it from the spare change in my pocket.

"But aren't either of you interested in politics?" Arlie protested. "Don't you think you ought to be?"

"Why in the name of heaven *ought* we to be?" Phoenix demanded.

"Because people like us have — well — more education than the average."

"You don't call a degree from this pile of pseudo-Gothic education, I hope!"

Arlie looked uncomfortable; he could never cope with Phoenix's sarcasm. I came to his rescue.

"You can't just go into politics, Arlie," I pointed out. "You can't just graduate from college and expect people to elect you to office. You have to do something first."

He looked at me with those wide, absolutely serious eyes.

"Do something? What?"

"Well, say, be a lawyer."

"Would I have to be a lawyer for long?"

He looked so upset that I relented.

"Not for too long."

"But you don't understand him, Peter," Phoenix broke

in with an air of false friendliness. "When he says 'people like us' he doesn't mean educated people. He doesn't mean you and me, either. He means people like his old man. *Rich* people. Rich as Crœsus. Rich as Kane!"

Poor Arlie flushed deeply.

"Shut up, Weld," he muttered.

"Shut up? Who do you think I am, your third valet?" Phoenix retorted. "I'll say what I want, fat butt. And when you get out of your Rolls-Royce to enter the halls of Congress remember one thing, just this — "

I was walking behind Phoenix, and I tripped him up. He stumbled and fell in the slush. Then he jumped up, furious, and started throwing snow at us. But he was too angry, and his aim was bad, and Arlie and I ran easily off to a safe distance. His voice, now a screech, came after us.

"Remember, Kane, you'll owe everything you get all your life to your old man's dough! *Everything* you get! Because you're as thick as mud, Arleus Kane! And everyone in school knows it!"

It was, as I have said, the end of the winter term, and everybody hated everybody. But Arlie made no allowance for seasonal moods. What he heard he took literally, and all during lunch that day he said almost nothing at all.

The following fall Arlie went to Harvard and I to Yale, and we saw much less of each other in the ensuing four years. I heard a great deal about him, however, for he became a well-known and popular figure in Boston and Cambridge, a position very different from the one he had occupied at school. Everyone who met him at Harvard, of course, knew just who he was, and his modesty about his money and family was considered charming. He began to go about, slightly dazzled but essentially unspoilt, with a very snappy crowd. Phoenix, who also went to Harvard and failed to make the club he wanted, was utterly disgusted with the whole thing. He and I had become, with the fading of school animosities, rather friendly, and he told me scornfully one weekend at a party in New York about the new Arlie Kane.

"Not that he's changed," he conceded. "I'll say that for old fat butt. He's the same innocent boob. But how people fawn on him! It's enough to make one a red. They're tickled to death to find a millionaire whom they can like without seeming to apple polish. You ought to hear the janitor in my entry. 'Mr. Kane's the fine young man,' he's always telling me. 'Nothing stuck up about him, no indeed. Just as simple as Jo the iceman!'"

I'm afraid I rather enjoyed listening to Phoenix's mean tongue. I suppose I was jealous that Arlie, who had been more or less my sort of person at school, should be catapulted into social prominence because of his money. There may even have been a mean little part of me that resented the fact that poor Arlie should consider, as I was afraid he might, that it was all due to his own charm and personality. When I thought about our conversation afterwards I was rather sorry about my part in it, but it proved to me, at any rate, that I was more conscious myself of Arlie's money than I had thought.

When I visited him on Long Island that summer, for example, there was a great deal of talk about a trip to Europe that he and some Harvard friends were taking. He asked me to go along with them, though the party was already made up, and I was touched and pleased, but it was unfortunately out of the question, as I couldn't afford it. When I explained this to him he nodded quickly, as he always did when the question of money came up, and dropped the matter immediately. But it occurred to me, even though I despised myself for thinking it and even though I wouldn't have accepted had he offered it, that he might have suggested a contribution to my expenses. He may have rejected the idea, of course, as presumptuous on his part and embarrassing for me. Or he may have been afraid of owing the least part of my friendship to gratitude. But there it was. I wanted to feel at least that he had thought of it.

It was during this visit that he showed his surprising interest in Phoenix.

"Do you think he'd come down here if I asked him?" he wanted to know.

I glanced from the flagstoned terrace on which we were sitting, down over the richly green, closely cut, sloping lawn to the blue of Long Island Sound.

"Would he come?" I repeated in surprise. "Would you ask him?"

"Why not?"

"But, Arlie, he's never been a friend of yours. He's never had a good word to say for you."

"That's just it," he said stubbornly, shaking his head. "That's why. Maybe if he came down here and stayed with me, he'd change his mind. He's awfully smart, you know. I hate to have him think the things he does."

"But at school you never cared what people thought, Arlie!"

"I did about some people. I always did."

I reflected a bit wryly that he would have probably been more interested in what I thought if I had hurt him, as Phoenix had, in his vulnerable spot. I was like the solid South: I could be taken for granted.

"I suppose it'll make you a good politician," I conceded. "Caring what people think. Are you still planning to go into politics, Arlie?"

"Oh, yes. I feel that more than ever." He nodded gravely. "I'm going to law school, too. Wouldn't it be fun if we ended up in the same law school, Peter? We might room together. Do you think we might?"

Which in fact two years later was just what happened. But then things had a way of turning out the way Arlie planned them. There was a simplicity about him that seemed to defy and temporarily to overcome the complications of the universe. Phoenix did go down to visit him and was rather embarrassed when he told me about it afterwards. He put it all quite crudely on the grounds of his own materialism, telling me that the Kanes, after all, had the biggest place on Long Island and the only decent shooting, but I knew it wasn't that. I knew he had been touched, if only for the moment, by Arlie's friendliness and was ashamed to admit it. When we ended up in the Yale Law School, we all three roomed together.

During law school summers Phoenix and I visited a lot at the Kanes' and went to far too many of the Long Island parties, dancing under marquees in the hot green dampness of June dawns, protected, at least I hoped, by the inevitable approach of war from the early prospect of dipping our heads below the surface of the ground to travel into eternity on our ceaseless way to and from the job downtown. For in New York the subway is the symbol of our bondage, the great mark of the essential leveler that the downtown world is. The rich young man like Arlie, after his brief fling under the Japanese lanterns, dancing until dawn in his white coat, obediently recognizes when his time is up and without a murmur, perhaps without a thought, like Huxley's sexagenarians before the gas chambers, joins his less privileged brothers in the crowded black cars of the Lexington Avenue line. Arlie, however, showed no disposition to protest his fate; he was full of enthusiasm about the prospect of a job with Everett & Coates in the fall after our graduation. It would, as he told me, satisfactorily fill in the gap between the end of his education and his first appearance on the political scene.

That summer was the period of his infatuation, if it isn't too strong a word, with Amanda Lorum. Amanda was conspicuously the most attractive girl in the Long Island world of the Kanes; she had wonderful black eyes and hair and a deep, rather desperate laugh that was considered pure Fitzgerald by the few who in that day still read him. She and Arlie were inseparable; they went out with a remorseless gaiety, unusual for him, to every party in the neighborhood and as they left, in the early hours of the morning, Amanda would pick up any stray friends walking down the drive to their cars and whisk them across the island, in Arlie's great green Cadillac, to swim in the surf or to sail with them on Long Island Sound. I liked Amanda, and I approved of her effect on Arlie. He seemed with her to have a bright, even a carefree manner which, no matter how clumsily he carried it off — and I concede it was clumsy — had more the appearance of youth and spontaneity than anything he had shown so far.

Amanda, who traveled, as I have indicated, with a very sophisticated group, had nonetheless her semi-serious side.

"I know you think Arlie's stuffy and a bore," she told me once, "but I wonder if one couldn't make something of him. Do you think one could?"

"I never said he was stuffy or boring," I retorted.

"Of course, you didn't *say* it. You're too stuffy yourself. But you think it. You look down on him in a smug, bourgeois way."

I said nothing.

"There!" she said triumphantly. "You said it again. But do you imagine I care what you think, Peter Westcott? Of course not. And do you know why? Because I wonder if I'm not in love with the guy. I really and honestly do."

"You wouldn't care, then, if he lost all his money?"

"Naturally, I'd care!" she exclaimed indignantly. "I'd care frightfully. But he couldn't, could he? Isn't there too much of it?"

"You think if you're frank you can be mercenary, Amanda," I warned her. "My sense of humor is too bourgeois for that."

"Now you're being tiresome. You see things so blackly and whitely. I'm simply not made that way. If I'm in love with Arlie Kane, it's because he's sweet and kind and serious. And because he has a big Cadillac, sure. I don't break him down into his component parts and decide which part I love him for. Arlie to me is a whole. Don't you see, Peter? His money is part of the charm, like perfume on a beautiful woman."

"Are you implying that money can have sex appeal?"

"But of course, you poor idiot! Terribly!"

"And you wouldn't marry him without it?"

She shrugged her shoulders.

"How should I know?" she asked impatiently. "Would I marry him if he lost a leg? Or all his hair? Or if he planned to live in Jersey City? Maybe I would. And maybe not. The only test is how I'd behave if any of those things happened *after* I married him. I can answer that one, Peter. I'd stick."

Whatever Amanda was, she was not a hypocrite. Not long after this conversation she must have had a similar one with Arlie, for their friendship broke up decisively just at the time that the rest of us were expecting the announcement of their engagement. Arlie told me about it at a dance, the last of the season and the biggest. Amanda had gone off suddenly to Maine, and he had spent the whole evening talking to a plain little girl with messy brown hair called Jennie Child. Toward the end of the party he took me aside to the bar, and we had a drink together.

"You're a friend of Amanda's, too," he said in his slow, direct way, looking down at the drink in his hands. "I thought I'd better tell you. That's all strictly in the past, Amanda and me."

"Oh. Should I be sorry?"

"Well, it's hit me pretty hard, Peter," he said, shaking his head, and I couldn't help wondering if it had. "But it's better to break it up now than later, don't you think?"

"I suppose. That is, if it has to be broken up."

He hesitated and took a long sip of his drink.

"She was after my chips, Peter," he said in his gravest tone, looking me straight in the eye and then away again.

After his chips. I had never heard him use that expression. But then I had never heard him refer to his money, certainly never in so serious a connection. My first thought was that I couldn't deny it. My second was one of sympathy for Amanda. For it occurred to me that she might, after all, have been in love with him.

"People are always after something in us that we may not regard as our greatest asset," I murmured with a touch of bitterness. "Would you rather she was after your blue eyes? Or your dimples?"

He looked shocked.

"You don't mean, Peter, that I shouldn't *mind*? When she practically told me to my face that she was in love with — with my money?"

I looked at his dismayed countenance and almost smiled. Poor Arlie.

"No," I said, putting my hand on his shoulder, "I wouldn't go that far. I suppose you should mind. I suppose you're right."

For how ever to explain to him that in Amanda self-awareness and honesty made a little fault, perhaps a universal one, loom large? It was no use. In families like the Kanes the greatest fear of all is the fear of being married for their money. It haunts them, for it is so hard to prevent. The simplest-looking girl, even of unimpeachable antecedents and comfortable means, may nonetheless harbor a design to marry for reasons dictated by the head and not the heart. And could such a creature ever be trained to believe, or even to act as if she believed, that a fortune was really a burden that one had to carry with courage? How Mrs. Kane had managed to implant this fear so firmly in Arlie and at the same time to teach him, as she had when he was small, that the Kanes were no different, no richer, really than anyone else, I don't know, but there was no question that she had succeeded. Arlie, so far as I could make out, never gave Amanda a second chance to explain herself.

Immediately after this he began to see Jennie Child in the same steady fashion that he had been seeing Amanda. He was determined, apparently, to get married before starting work; I suspect that he regarded marriage as a kind of clean, sweet-smelling cedar box, provided to each young man on the completion of his education, in which he was meant to check his emotional appetites before embarking on the long usefulness of his career. I have often wondered if Jennie, when she came to open the cedar box, found it as full as it should have been. Perhaps, though, it didn't matter. For Jennie was almost as great an heiress as Arlie was an heir and had been raised in the same tradition, with the exception that less was expected of her, being a girl. She had been allowed to grow up converting her principles into athletic prowess, her democratic ideals into long days on horseback in blue jeans on her father's

Arizona ranch, her good fellowship into a rather violent love of domestic animals. Her romance with Arlie was as wholesome and filling as a breakfast food after the brief but distressing interlude of Amanda. Each of them could comfortably reflect that whatever the other's motivation, it was not mercenary.

They were married in the fall after our graduation and settled in a small apartment in New York, obeying the firmest of rules among people like the Kanes and Childs that a young married couple must go through a probation period of appearing to live on what the husband earns. It is a sort of ceremonial, a brief bow of the head, an almost reverent recognition of other lives and other conditions. It ends with the birth of the first baby, after which everything, the nurse or nurses, the place in the country, the camp in Maine, the general expansion of life with further babies to include cars and boats and even planes, is always done "for the children," until the parents themselves have reached middle age and can at last be frankly richer than their neighbors and drive in a limousine behind a chauffeur who is no longer disguised as the children's tutor.

The probation period, however, was cut short for Arlie, as he needed money in his political activities. For he actually did go into politics. I suppose the only reason I regarded this as surprising was that he had always planned it, and it seemed astonishing to me that anyone could so literally carry out, much less want to carry out, a childhood plan. But Arlie had no revulsion such as mine against his early concepts. He never regarded himself as a different person at different ages, which gave to his life an extraordinary consistency. The evenings that he did not spend at Everett & Coates, where I also was working, he now spent at meetings and rallies. He had chosen to be a Democrat, a phenomenon more common with the very rich than with the rich, and he talked gravely and interminably to all who would listen about the social changes brought about by the New Deal, as if they had not already become established historical facts, and advocated intervention in the war that had started in Europe as if the Nazi threat was his private discovery.

I confess that I was inclined to be rather irritable with Arlie at this period. Part of it, I suppose, was a feeling of guilt that I was doing nothing at all about being a good citizen while he girded his loins for greater things. But it wasn't entirely guilt. There was also the exasperation of being tied down to a job that I didn't really like, an impatient horse in a long dark stable, and seeing Arlie, who could have been out in the fields, the woods, anywhere, meekly and contentedly chewing his hay in the adjoining stall. I would get angry with him and pretend to be violently isolationist or reactionary to shock him, but it only resulted in his going over for the hundredth time the tired and incontestable clichés that bolstered his point of view in everything. Arlie believed that everyone could be convinced by logic, even people who didn't want to be.

"Why don't you go over there?" I asked one day in exasperation, as he started to tell me again why England was our first line of defense and what we had always owed to the Royal Navy. "You could get there as a war correspondent, couldn't you? If you care so much, why not see it for yourself?"

"There's the little matter of my job," he pointed out blandly.

"Throw it up. What's a job, anyway?"

"Most people seem to find them useful."

"Most people aren't you, Arlie."

He looked away from me in that evasive way that he had whenever reference was made to his money.

"Take a chance, Arlie," I protested. "Why be a hack all your life just because everyone else is? Hell, there's no virtue in that. We're going to get into this war soon enough, thanks to guys like you. Why not enjoy yourself in the meantime?"

His lips tightened, and I could see I had offended him.

"You're not in a good mood today, Peter," he said quietly. "Otherwise you'd see that there's not much point in my leading the life that *you*'d like. Besides, I've got commitments. I'm going to run for the Assembly."

I gaped. I suppose, like Phoenix, I had never really believed that anyone would run him for anything.

"You always seem to have the last word, Arlie," I said, shaking my head with a rather shamefaced admiration. "I suppose it could be that you deserve it. Good luck, old man. Here's one vote you can count on."

He lost the election, which was a foregone conclusion, as his district was solidly Republican, but everyone conceded that he had campaigned with a notable conscientiousness. I heard him speak only once. It was at a block party which he gave in his street, and he read his speech aloud from the back of a sound truck, in a high, careful voice, going into each issue in rather laborious fashion, with one hand nervously adjusting his glasses and the other raised in the air, the forefinger pointing to the sky. The crowd, mostly neighborhood, was curious, amused and, on the whole, friendly. The beer and pretzels, served in enormous quantities, also made their impression. I saw only one disagreeable person in the street, and that, of course, was Phoenix. He was bitterer than ever at this point in our lives; he had decided not to practice law and was writing a play about incest that he refused to show anyone. Hailing me from a distance, he walked unsteadily across the street to join me. He was very drunk and was making fun of the small group of Arlie's enthusiasts.

"Do you know Arleus Kane?" he asked me in a loud voice. "Isn't he the greatest guy you ever knew? Isn't he gracious? Don't you admire the simple, unaffected way he speaks to the people? Do you know what he called me just now? He called me 'Phoenix.' My own Christian name. Just plain Phoenix. No lugs about him, no sirree. Nothing hoity-toity about Arlie Kane."

I turned away, disgusted at last with Phoenix and the part of myself that I finally saw in him. For Arlie's fortune, however we minimized it, had created a problem and a problem that was not his alone. It was a problem for Amanda and Jennie, for myself and Phoenix, and nothing was clearer, as I walked away, trying to forget the spite in the latter's face, that, for all his clumsiness, Arlie alone among us was trying to face it.

WALLY

WALLY

THE WINTER OF 1942 WAS A BAD TIME FOR MOST OF US
stationed in the American Naval Intelligence Office in
Balboa, Canal Zone. In the first place, all work of any
importance was handled either by G-2, the Army Intelligence unit, or by the Civilian Intelligence Agency of
the Zone, leaving us with nothing to do but file and refile
thousands of blue and yellow cards, which had been sent
down from Washington on the remote chance that one of
the suspects whose names were on the cards might journey
to Panama to blow up the Canal. In the second place, and
more important, most of the younger officers felt very
guilty about not being at sea, because at the time we
seemed to be losing the war. We had applied for intelligence commissions before Pearl Harbor, mainly because
they were easy to get and would enable us to avoid the
draft; we had not reflected that we might be disqualifying
ourselves for a combat part in the future. Now all we
could do was forward to the Bureau of Personnel applications for sea duty bearing the endorsement "Not Approved" by our district intelligence officer, Commander
Carter, who, although sympathetic, was far too good a
bureaucrat to allow his office to be stripped of men by any

such scruples as ours. So day after day we moped in the dampness and heat of the tropical Isthmus, doing puzzles in office hours and drinking heavily in the long cool evenings at the Union Club or El Rancho, until we became drugged into a listless discontent and almost dreaded the very change that we spent our time trying to believe we craved.

There were two officers in the younger group, however, who had no wish to go to sea. Of these, Ensign Wallingford, known as Wally, was the franker and more vociferous. He came from Omaha, and carried emotional isolationism to a degree I have never seen equalled. He not only wanted no part of the war; he wanted no part of *anything* outside America. As for Panama, the Zone, and the people there — even the least possibility of personal broadening — he rejected them all, and performed his daily chores in a bleak, grudging way. Each of the senior officers, including those who barely acknowledged the existence of ensigns, came to know and deplore him, with his small slim figure, his crew cut, which made his features seem so large, and his sullen, flushed face, dominated by thick lips and a projecting jaw. For it was Wally who managed to smash up Commander Carter's station wagon when carrying dispatches to G-2 and who collided with the Chief of Staff in the vestibule of our office building, causing his tropical hat to roll across the floor like a big brown crazy egg while a Marine orderly chased frantically after it. Wally was convinced that the world was in conspiracy against him, and I could read in his black eyes a smug little pride that it was he, after all, who was causing his superiors the most trouble.

"I've just put in my third application for a transfer," he told me grimly one evening at the officer's bar. "My third in four months. I'll keep at it, though. They'll see."

"Disapproved, of course."

"Naturally."

"Did you apply for hotels again?" I asked, with a smile. Wally was a graduate of the Cornell hotel school.

"Of course!" he exclaimed. "The Navy's taking over hotels all over the country. They *need* people like me. How can they expect to win a total war if they don't use people for what they've been trained?"

"Nonsense," I retorted. "How can everyone possibly do what they've been trained to do? How many of us were trained to fight?"

He shook his head several times, slowly and soberly. "There are plenty of people to do the fighting," he said. "It takes more than fighting to win a war. It takes organization."

"I suppose you think it's wasteful of the Navy not to use me in legal work?"

"Oh, no. There are plenty of lawyers," he said. "There's no need for more of them. But how many people are there who know how to run a hotel dining room?"

I threw my hands in the air. "You're too good for this war, Wally, is that it? Too good to be wasted in Panama? Too good to go to sea?"

"That's one way of looking at it," he said blandly. "But it's not the nice way. Anyhow, we'll probably both be here till it's all over. If it ever is over, that is — the way they're going about it in Washington."

I was stung by his prediction, for it reminded me of the unpleasant likelihood that, whatever our respective states of mind, Wally's and my war duties and futures would be identical. If he had ever conceded that my naval ambitions were even slightly more public-spirited than his, I would have been mollified, but he had never done this. He thought I was theatrical, or even hypocritical, in protesting that I wanted to go to sea.

Even more provoking was the point of view of the other of our two shore-duty enthusiasts, Lieutenant (j.g.) Sherwood Lane. Sherwood had been in the Zone fourteen months — a good deal longer than the rest of us — and he quite seriously believed that this tour of duty entitled him to a transfer to Washington, where his experience, which he felt had been painfully acquired, could be used in some executive capacity. But so far he hadn't put in an application. A desire for shore duty at home was, however, the only point he had in common with Wally. Where Wally was often as stubborn and morose as a peasant, Sherwood was entirely the aristocrat. His manners, especially toward his seniors, were impeccable. Tall and suave, he wore his prematurely graying hair in a crew cut and had a twinkle in his eyes that made you think at first he had a sense of humor. He also possessed a booming laugh, which he saved for Commander Carter's jokes, and a large red Cadillac convertible, which he drove to the office every morning — a distance of less than a quarter of a mile from his living quarters — stopping on the way to pick up the Admiral's secretary. On Saturday nights, he always reserved a table in the bar of the Union Club, with two ice buckets and constantly replenished champagne; it became a rendezvous for the higher-ranking naval officers of the district and for ships in Balboa for supplies or repair. Sherwood made a particular show of "nothing but the best" for the boys who were on their way to the Pacific. Incredible as it seemed, he regarded their first and possibly most arduous assignment as the transit of the Canal itself.

"The people at home simply don't know what we're going through," he told me one night at the Union Club, following his return from a short leave in the States. He had just ordered his car, because he was going on to a party. "Admiral Anderson, the chief of my home naval district, asked me to speak to the men at his headquarters. They all showed up, too, about two hundred of them. Maybe they were told to, I don't know about that, but I'm not kidding when I say you could have heard a pin drop while I was talking. Oh, they're good kids and willing to learn, there's no question about that. But somebody's *got* to tell them."

"You don't have a copy of that speech, do you?" I asked, with a straight face. "I'd love to read it. I really would."

"No, I'm sorry. I spoke from notes. It was just the idea of getting across the notion that outside their precious borders there's a war going on."

"Did you tell them about Wally and his hotel applications?" I couldn't help asking.

He looked perplexed, and I was afraid for a moment that I had gone too far. "Now, why in the name of God would I want to tell anyone about that little squirt?"

"Oh, I just thought it might have added local color."

"Local color that I can do without, thank you," he said. "You know something? That guy is more than just a bad joke. He's a disgrace to the service. He does nothing but scheme all day to fix himself up with a soft spot at home."

I had to hide my face in my glass.

"Of course, I'm not saying I wouldn't like a tour of duty at home myself," Sherwood admitted. "But our cases are as different as day and night. I've been overseas for fourteen months and learned a couple of things they might find useful in Washington."

"Of course you have," I agreed, emerging from my glass. "It's only a question of fitting in where one can be most useful."

Wally might have continued his scheming, as Sherwood called it, to no effect had he not come up with a fantastic plan, which he revealed to me one morning in the office. He apparently trusted me sufficiently to seek my advice. I stared at a letter that he proudly laid on my desk. It was nothing less than a direct appeal, over the head of Commander Carter, to Admiral Terence, the Commandant:

FROM: *Clark Wallingford, Ensign USNR.*
TO: *Commandant, Fifteenth Naval District.*
SUBJECT: *Duty appropriate to rank and station, request for.*
1. The Commandant is respectfully advised that Ensign Wallingford has been attached to the District Intelligence Office for six months, during which time he has been engaged in checking the daily passenger lists of commercial aircraft against the suspect cards in the Intelligence Office's files. This duty never occupies Ensign Wallingford for

more than an hour a day and usually less.
2. It is respectfully requested that Ensign Wallingford be assigned duties commensurate with his rank and station and in accordance with his prior applications for change of duty.

I gazed up at him for a moment, and then, picking up the document, I reached over and let it fall gently into the wastebasket.

"Now in the hands of the action addressee," I said firmly.

"Don't do that!" Wally retrieved the letter hastily, and with an anxious eye looked it over for wrinkles. "I'm going to put it in."

"You're going to do no such thing!"

"Certainly I am. Why shouldn't I?"

"Because it's just plain crazy," I said impatiently. "Besides, you haven't gone through the chain of command."

He sniffed. "A fat lot of good that's ever done me. I want to make sure the Admiral reads this. He never reads anything that Carter disapproves."

"But how will you even get it to him?"

"I'll put it in his in-basket when he's at lunch."

I gaped. "The yeoman will stop you. You can't just throw miscellaneous papers on the Admiral's desk."

"I've got it all figured out. I'll slip it in when the yeoman's at the Coke machine."

His face was deadly earnest, and I felt suddenly that I was dealing with a man who had lost his reason. "Wally," I said, "you can't do it. They'll hang you!"

"How can they?" he demanded. "It's out of order, but

it's not a court-martial offense. I'm making a personal appeal to Admiral Terence, that's all. *He* ought to be interested in the waste of officer personnel in his own district!"

"But, Wally — " I pleaded, and then gave up, knowing how stubborn he could be, most of all when he felt that right was on his side.

"Well, I warned you," I said. "Don't ever say I didn't warn you!"

Even Wally weakened after he had actually done the deed that day at noon. He had a wild impulse to retrieve his letter, he told me, but when he ran up again to the Admiral's floor, he froze at the sight, through the doorway, of the familiar gray head behind the desk. He was too late. We dined together that night at a small restaurant in Panama City, feeling like a couple of conspirators. After two drinks, Wally's face began to grow pink with concern.

"They'll send me out to the Pacific," he said. "That's what they'll do. In a submarine or a PT boat."

"They don't use ships for punishment, Wally."

"That's what *you* think. Have you ever been on one?"

I let this go by.

"There's a professor from the hotel school who's a lieutenant commander," he continued gloomily. "He's been sent to Miami to run the hotels there for the subchaser school. Do you think if I wrote him he could fix it up in Washington to get me as his assistant?"

"They censor that stuff, you know," I said. Commander Carter had made especially stringent rules for the Intelligence Office. Even informal requests for change of duty had to be deleted from our correspondence.

"But if I did it on a day when you were censoring the mail?" he suggested, looking at me hopefully.

That was going too far. "It would have to be censored just the same," I said.

He looked down at the table with a depressed expression. "Okay," he said. "Don't rub it in. I thought you might be a friend, that's all."

"I have to obey orders, Wally."

"Oh, that." He sighed, as if he would never come to the end of the hypocrisy in the world. "You've got it in for me because I don't want to go to sea. You're as bad as the rest."

Wally didn't get sent to the Pacific. The following afternoon, Commander Carter was summoned to the Commandant's office, and when he returned, he had a long conference with his two division heads. This was followed by a good deal of whispering among the senior officers. The story, as I got it from Sherwood while we stood in the office corridor by the Coca-Cola machine, was that a request by Commander Carter, in the best bureaucratic tradition, for twenty additional officers had been lying on top of the Admiral's in-basket when Wally slipped in his private communication. The Admiral had read them both together. Fortunately for all concerned, he had been primarily amused. "Put your people to work, Carter," he had said gruffly, and had torn up both documents.

"Poor Wally," I said. "Carter will really have it in for him now."

"Just between you and me and the lamppost, Carter's already consulted me on how to get rid of him," Sherwood told me, glancing discreetly from one side to the other to see if anyone might be listening.

"I shouldn't think that was so hard," I retorted. "All Carter has to do is approve one of his hotel applications."

Sherwood looked startled. "And give him the very thing he wants!" he exclaimed. "After what he's done to the Commander! Not on your life, boy. You don't know the Regular Navy."

"What will you do with him, then?"

Sherwood shrugged casually. "I'll think up something. Don't worry."

For the first time I began to be irritated, and not amused, by Sherwood. "How does it feel to be the Commander's hatchet man?" I asked.

But Sherwood, as I might have known, took this almost as a compliment. "Not the kind of thing I like to get into as a rule, of course," he answered, lowering his voice, "but frankly in this case I don't mind. That little jerk has been asking for it ever since he arrived. He makes the rest of us look as idiotic as he is! What if my application for staff duty hit BuPers on the same day as one of those ridiculous whimpers of his about hotels? Do you think I'd have a chance?"

I had wondered for some time why Sherwood disliked Wally so much. Now I understood. Wally, who didn't care if the other officers thought him selfish to want shore duty, held up a cruel mirror to Sherwood's concept of his own role in the war. Sherwood could never afford to be bracketed with Wally. Seeing how dangerous this attitude could be for Wally, I was on the verge of pointing out that to give him what he wanted, however distasteful to Carter, would at least get rid of him faster than anything else, when the Admiral's secretary came up to get a coke, and Sherwood turned away from me.

Wally's letter to the Admiral, as it happened, affected all our lives. For only a week later the Admiral received a Bureau of Personnel directive about the need for additional officers at sea, and, evidently remembering Ensign Wallingford's description of his duties, he requested his secretary to find out how many intelligence officers were actually required at headquarters. This was followed, after what must have been a painful week indeed for Commander Carter, by an order saying that all applications for sea duty would now be favorably endorsed.

When all of us who applied were summoned to Commander Carter's office one morning, I was surprised to see Wally in the group. He was wearing his dampest, most suspicious look.

"Have you had a change of heart?" I whispered to him. "Have you lost faith in the hotel as the highroad to victory?"

He ignored this. "It's that son of a bitch, Sherwood Lane," he said. "He's trying to railroad me out of here. That's why he stuck my name on the list. He thinks I won't dare back out. Well, he'll see."

Sitting at his desk, upon which were little gray models of battleships and cruisers — the miniature Pacific in which he liked to play — the Commander addressed us. "I want to tell you gentlemen," he said pleasantly, "that I am now prepared to endorse your applications. I've always had the greatest sympathy with your desire to serve your country at sea, and I'm tickled to death to be able to do something about it at last. If you are taken, it will mean, of course, that extra work will fall upon the shoulders of those who are left, but this is war, gentlemen, and we are up to it. Good luck to you."

I was almost touched by this, for he seemed to mean it. We all murmured our thanks except Wally, who moved slowly forward, his sullen gaze intent upon the Commander.

"Does that mean me, sir?"

Commander Carter looked up at Wally. "Why, yes, Wally," he said, with a forced smile. "You're going to sea! And if you only knew how I envy you, too! Gee, man, to think, after twenty years in the Navy, when we finally get into a real scrap, I have to be moored to a desk — "

"But I don't want to go to sea!"

There was a terrible silence. "I beg your pardon?" the Commander said.

"I don't want to go to sea!" Wally repeated indignantly. "I never applied for sea duty. The others did, not me!"

He was so absorbed in the injustice of it that he appeared to have utterly forgotten where he was. He was leaning forward, one hand resting squarely on the Commander's desk, his black eyes fixed on his superior officer.

"Do you mean to stand there in a naval uniform and tell me you won't go to sea?" the Commander thundered. "Why, it ought to be stripped off you this minute!"

"It's all because I wrote that letter to the Admiral," Wally muttered.

"Get out of this office!" the Commander said. "Get out immediately!"

I knew now that Wally's case was desperate. One simply does not violate the naval convention that those "on the beach" must continually express preference for duty afloat. I decided that afternoon, in Wally's interest, to call on Sherwood in his room, and I found him very righteous indeed about the scene in Carter's office.

"Imagine his saying a thing like that in front of the Commander!" he exclaimed as he poured me a drink. "Who would have thought even a nut like Wallingford would have dared?"

"I almost admired him for it."

"You didn't!"

"It was the only way he could foil your little plan, and he knew it. He wasn't going to be shanghaied into going to sea. Not Wally."

"Oh, yes? Well, in that case he made a mistake," Sherwood said. "Where he's going will make sea duty seem sweet. God in heaven, man, it's not enough that he makes a fool of Carter before the Commandant, that he strips our office of half the officers! He's got to insult the Navy itself!" There was something almost hysterical now in Sherwood's need to destroy Wally.

"What are you going to do with him?" I asked.

"Galápagos Islands," he snapped. "Assistant naval observer. We'll see how he likes that for a year or so. Of course, it's a bit lonely," he continued with a sneer, "but our Wally is hardly the social type."

"Can't you let him be?" I said angrily. "Can't you leave

the poor guy alone? Why crucify him?"

Sherwood stared at me. "You mean you actually care what happens to that little squirt?"

"Sure I care. He's a friend of mine."

He laughed incredulously. "Tell that to the Marines. What's eating you, anyway?"

"I'll tell you what's eating me," I said hotly. "You want to ship him out of here so you can put in your own precious application! It burns me up, Lane!"

"Why, you can't think that!" he protested, jumping up. "Didn't I tell you that Commander Carter himself told me to arrange about this? And don't you know the only reason I want to go to Washington —"

But I had already started out the door. I went straight to Wally's room, in an adjoining building, and found him stretched out on the bed in his shorts, wearing an eyeshade. He looked small and white and worn out.

"Wally," I said abruptly, "you remember about that officer friend of yours in Miami?"

He sat up slowly and took off his eyeshade. "What about him?" he asked, blinking.

"Write him," I said. "Write him at once. And give the letter to me."

He jumped out of bed. "You mean it? You really will? Where's my pen? Wait, I'll do it right now."

Very much to my surprise, the letter got results. Maybe there was something in Wally's theory, after all, that the Navy needed officers with hotel training. Maybe the lieutenant commander saw qualities in him that we did not see in Panama. Or maybe it was just luck. At any rate, his orders came barely ten days after the letter was dispatched and just before the Galápagos plan was completed. He was borne safely off into the sky in a Navy patrol plane. When he was leaving, he was so excited — and so terrified at the possibility of a cancellation of orders — that he scarcely took time to say goodbye to me. I was a bit disgusted at his exaltation, at the utterness of his failure to see himself as anything but the happily escaped victim of evil men.

"Good luck, Wally," I said. "There'll probably be a fire in your hotel and you'll save everybody. Yes, I can see it. You'll be a hero in spite of yourself."

Wally, it turned out, spent the rest of the war in a hotel in Miami, performing, unheroically, the tasks for which he considered himself adequately trained. This, of course, was predictable. What was not predictable was what happened to Sherwood after Wally and the rest of us left. His application for duty in Washington was accepted, and after a few months in the Navy Department he applied for a course in combat intelligence. Having completed this, he was assigned to a carrier in the Pacific, where he spent two years. Just before the end of the war, I heard that he had been awarded the Silver Star.

Toward the end of the war, I ran into Commander Carter, then a captain and the skipper of a transport, at an officers' club in Leyte. I asked him how he could explain what must have been a total change of attitude on Sherwood's part.

His answer was simple. "I know it's a phrase you reserves don't like," he told me as he poured himself a stiff drink from my one precious bottle of bourbon, "but it still seems to me to sum up a lot of things. That phrase is 'officer and gentleman.' Sherwood may have been a spoiled brat, I grant. He was probably a mama's darling when he was little, and, of course, he had his pompous side. But fundamentally he was an officer and a gentleman. That's what you can't get away from, my friend, and don't you forget it. Wallingford, of course, was neither."

Well, it could have been the answer. I shrugged. But I couldn't escape the idea that Wally had motivated Sherwood, as in some degree, perhaps, he had motivated the rest of us. None of us, least of all Sherwood, could really stand to live for any length of time with that part of ourselves we recognized in Wally.

LOYALTY UP
AND
LOYALTY DOWN

Loyalty Up and Loyalty Down

I N NOVELS ABOUT NAVAL LIFE IN WORLD WAR II, THE COM-
manding officer of a ship usually emerges as a heel or a
hero, as a Captain Queeg (*The Caine Mutiny*), for example, or a Captain Ericson (*The Cruel Sea*). In point of
fact, of course, the commanding officer was frequently a
small-minded, rather pathetic man, incapable of wielding
his unwanted authority without constantly justifying himself by harrying others over minor tasks. This type rarely
draws more than passing attention today — probably, I
suspect, because the dislike and anger that he inspired in
his subordinates has now been forgotten or lost in a sort
of mild pity. We shrug smugly and wonder how we ever
could have felt so strongly about him; if we meet him in
the street, we hail him cheerfully and offer to buy him a
drink.

Such a man was Harry Ellis, the skipper of the LST
1301, whose executive officer I was for almost a year. I
was transferred to his ship in 1943, and during the time I
was aboard, we were engaged, along with other LSTs, in
a ferry service between Nouméa and Guadalcanal and
other islands in the New Hebrides and the Solomons.
Ellis was a handsome man in his early thirties, with thick,

curly, blond hair — which he constantly fingered to keep in place — that made him seem younger than he was. He wore a gold watch on one wrist and a silver identification tag on the other, and his gestures showed how conscious he was of them. He had enlisted in the Navy at seventeen and had worked up to chief boatswain's mate when the war broke out. Soon afterward, he had been commissioned, quite against his will, a senior lieutenant, and just before I was assigned to him, he had received his first command.

At the start, I hoped that we might get on together. He seemed amiable, even easygoing, and immediately delegated to me the running of the ship, as a good commanding officer should, while he lay on his bunk and read detective stories. He would saunter up to the bridge, looking very dapper, when we left or entered port, and his ship handling, although theatrical, was not too much worse than that of the other LST skippers. When he did pull a *gaffe*, as when he knocked over the LST water pier in Espíritu Santo, leaving it a mass of broken, spurting pipes, he so filled the air with his complaints and excuses that the officers who investigated the accident were almost convinced that it had not been his fault. Ellis could even make himself liked when he wanted to. The trouble on our ship was that he never wanted to enough to bridge the gap between himself and the other officers.

There were really two gaps. One was that the other officers were all college graduates. They were civilians first and officers second, and they were also rather serious young men. Two of them had been, like me, lawyers before the war. Another, who planned to become a priest, insisted on

contributing twenty-five cents to the ship's welfare fund
every time he caught himself using a swearword. A fourth
had been a Latin teacher at a New England boys' boarding
school. The atmosphere of the wardroom was thus not
one that Ellis, with his rich fund of tales of liberty in tropical ports, found congenial. He was surprised and hurt
that his jokes were not better received, and soon suspicious
that we were looking down on him because he hadn't been
to college or because he was a former enlisted man. This
was unfair. What we looked down on, and it was responsible for the more serious of the two gaps between us,
was the meanness of his attitude toward the war. To him,
it was simply another episode in his twenty-year hitch, to
be got through with the least possible variation from pre-
war routine. He saw the ship herself as a reluctant loan
by the Navy to the Pacific Theater — one that must be
returned at all costs, intact and ready for a white-gloved
admiral's inspection. To save everything and to do the
minimum was not simply smart, he believed; it was meri-
torious. If a ship asked us, for instance, for fuel or water,
he would signal back, regardless of the level in our tanks,
that we were low ourselves. When other LSTs had to take
barges in tow, he would avoid doing this, on the claim of
a defective stern anchor winch. He would fake engine
trouble to avoid berthing at night, and as we were constantly being rerouted from Lunga Point to Tulagi or
from Henderson Creek to Purvis Bay, and rarely operated
for more than a couple of months under the same group
commander, it was possible for him to get away with these
things. Ellis didn't, of course, regard himself as getting

away with anything. He sincerely believed that he was behaving as a conscientious naval officer should behave.

Worst of all was his treatment of the small craft, such as LCTs, that were used for minor ferrying from island to island. As they never went back to Nouméa or Espíritu Santo, they had to depend for their supplies on the LSTs and larger ships, but, being outside the naval requisition-and-paper orbit, they were without redress, practically speaking, when refused. They wandered about in the anchorages, going from ship to ship, their crews sloppy, unshaven, finally sullen or, at times, even savage, living a scavenger life. Ellis would automatically refuse them anything but canned beans. The only way I could get anything to them was by smuggling it over the side when he wasn't on deck, and eventually he caught me at it.

I was supervising a forbidden unloading party on the fantail, one morning before breakfast, with Bob Horner, our gunnery officer, when Ellis appeared unexpectedly through the hatch that led to the ship's office. From where he was standing, however, he could not see that there were two LCVPs bobbing in the water below us, and I turned to him with the most innocent expression I could muster. He strolled toward me, his hands in his pockets, apparently in a good mood.

"What a beautiful morning it is," he said gaily. "I should think it's a day that even a Wall Street lawyer could enjoy. How about it, Mr. W.?"

"It is a beautiful day, Captain."

"You're not too learned, I take it, to appreciate the simple things of life?"

"Not at all, Captain."

"The simple things like myself, for instance?"

"Like yourself, sir."

He laughed loudly and, for him, pleasantly. "And what about you, Mr. Horner?"

"I share Mr. W.'s simple tastes, Captain."

"What about eggs? Have you got any fresh eggs?"

This last, regrettably, was not from Ellis. It boomed up from a sailor in one of the LCVPs below. There was an awkward silence, and then Ellis stepped quickly to the rail.

"Hey, you! What are you doing down there?" he called angrily. "That's all, now! Shove off! I say, shove off!"

The LCVPs, sizing up the situation, departed quietly — grateful, I hoped, for what they had already got.

Ellis whirled on me, in front of the deckhands. "I thought my orders were clear, Mr. W.," he said bitingly. "I thought no fresh supplies were to go to small craft."

"It's our responsibility to supply them, sir," I answered "I can show you the directive."

"I'll tell you what your responsibilities are," he shouted, getting very red. "Do you think you can boss this whole ship just because you went to Harvard?"

"Yale," I said softly.

"You think you're smart, don't you?" he sneered. "If you were really smart, you'd think of our own men before giving everything away to every ragamuffin in the harbor!"

He glanced around at the deckhands, actually appealing for their support. They remained expressionless.

"I thought we were all fighting the same war, sir," I said

stubbornly. "Ragamuffins, as you call them, *and* Harvard men."

"Don't talk back to me!" he shouted. "Go to your cabin!"

His appeal to the deckhands that day, ridiculous as it was, was understandable. He sought, however vainly, from the crew, who never knew the extent to which he shirked his duties, the support his officers withheld. It was only natural, it still seems to me, that we should have withheld it. We were humiliated by his conduct, and embarrassed to be serving on a ship that was not doing her part. He thought our attitude was priggish and essentially snobbish, as though a desire to co-operate with others in supplying the islands was one of those hollow, tinny ideals dished out in colleges like Harvard and maybe even Annapolis, to be used as instruments to keep people like himself in their places. He focused the bulk of his resentment on me, his executive officer and theoretically the administrator of his policy, and as his temper soured under the monotony of our trips, I became the target of all his unvarying humor.

"Tell them we're sorry, we have none to spare," he would say to the messenger who interrupted our meal with a request for machinery parts from a neighboring ship, "unless, of course, Mr. W. here, our Wall Street lawyer, will supply them out of his own personal store. Oh, he won't? You disapprove of my manners, don't you, Mr. W.? It isn't what you were taught at Harvard?"

"No, Captain."

"Well, I didn't have the privilege of attending one of those fancy institutions."

"We know that, Captain."

"Oh, you do? It must be so evident, mustn't it? I'm so sorry, so dredfawlly, dredfawlly sorry." He would wave his hand at me in a parody, as he saw it, of the effeminate and highborn. "But don't worry. In ten years, this horrid war will be over and you can run home to dear Mama, who will protect you from unrefined persons."

To do him justice, I don't think he had any conception of how galling such remarks could be when repeated meal after meal, month after month. He would say what to us were unforgivable things and then wonder afterward why, when he invited us to play gin rummy, or to go ashore with him, or even to have a secret drink in his cabin, he was invariably refused. We left him more and more out of the wardroom conversation, until he could dominate the table only with a harangue, to which we would listen in silence.

"Harvard men," he would mutter when he had finished haranguing us and we had resumed our discussion of books or politics, of law or religion — anything so long as he didn't know enough about it to join in. "God-damned fancy-pants Harvard men."

Oh, we were petty, yes, but pettiness was our only weapon against him. I can see now that we gave more than we got and that he must have found our organized hostility harder to live with than we found his foolish cracks about colleges. If I had shown him any affection, any kindliness, I might have changed the situation. But I would rather have died. My hostility had become my sole integrity.

The incident of the Marines shut the door on any conceivable rapprochement between Ellis and me. Our ship ferried back to New Caledonia the survivors of a regiment

of Marines who had been fighting for six weeks in the hills
of Bougainville, in almost impenetrable jungle. All of us
except Ellis were honored to have them aboard; he detested
them. He detested all passengers, on the theory that they
messed up the ship. The second morning they were aboard,
I was in the ship's office playing checkers with the yeoman,
Tolman, when the senior Marine officer, Major Frazer,
came running in. He told me that a man dressed in a
Chinese robe had stalked into the wardroom while his
officers were drinking coffee and had called them "pigs in
a pigsty." Luckily for the man, he had disappeared before
they had sufficiently recovered from their amazement to
grab him.

"Why, that must have been the Captain," I said, in a
tone of mild surprise. Ellis frequently wandered about
the wardroom in a red silk kimono, a relic of travels to
China. "Haven't they met him before? I didn't know he
spent that much time in his sack."

The Major stared. "The Captain! Is that the way commanding officers dress at sea?"

"Not all of them, of course not," I replied. "Very few
skippers are as well turned out as Captain Ellis."

"Well, this may be a great joke to you," the Major
snorted, "but those fellows are sore."

I reflected a moment or two. "Pig," I said, looking at the
yeoman. "I think that's one thing the Captain has never
called me. Have you ever heard him call me a pig, Tolman?"

"No, sir. An ox, sir. A dumb ox. Never a pig."

The Major looked belligerently from Tolman to me.

"Well, if your Captain wants to stay out of trouble," he snapped, "he'd better not go round insulting my officers. I can't guarantee what'll happen to someone who calls them pigs. Captain or no Captain."

"It would be terrible if anything happened to the Captain," I said. "Just terrible."

"Oh, all right," the Major said in disgust. "If you won't be serious, to hell with you!"

He was about to slam out of the office when I stood up. "Major," I said, taking him by the arm, "wait. Would an apology make them feel any better?"

"An apology? From the Captain?"

"No, I'm afraid I can't arrange that. From me."

The Major seemed uncomfortable. "Oh, I couldn't ask you to do that," he said. "After all, *you* didn't say anything to them."

"Where are they?" I asked. "In the wardroom?"

I went out of the office and down the passageway to the wardroom followed by the now bewildered Major. My heart was thumping, and I knew if I was going to do it, I would have to do it right away.

"Gentlemen," I said to the row of faces that turned to me as I entered the room, "the Major has informed me that you have just been insulted by the Captain of this ship. As executive officer, I should like to state that the Captain was voicing only his own opinion. On behalf of the officers and crew, I offer you an apology. You can be sure we are proud to have you on board."

I felt rather exalted after this and didn't much care whether or not Ellis found out. What, after all, could he do? Any report to higher authority would involve an explanation of his own atrocious manners, and as to the thousand and one mean little ways that a skipper can get back at one of his officers — well, I had seen them all, at least all that he was capable of. Fortunately, as I have already said, he was no Queeg.

He found out all right, just how I never knew, but beyond a few oblique remarks about loyalty he said nothing to me. Actually, I don't think he really minded. The incident had cleared the air, and we both knew where we stood. He was more interested, anyway, in a brisk business that he was engaged in of exchanging his liquor ration for perfume and cognac, which were still available in Nouméa, and for those big, floppy, hoop-skirted dolls that one sees in the windows of French dressmakers. He had a funny craze for the dolls and sat them up on the chairs and couch in his cabin, the atmosphere of which, thanks also to the inexpungeable scent of a bottle of perfume he had accidentally broken, had become peculiarly unnaval.

I had almost resigned myself to the bleak prospect of spending the rest of the war under Ellis's command when we were suddenly ordered to Pearl Harbor. We sailed jubilantly from Tulagi in a convoy of twelve LSTs, on a voyage that was to take thirty days — longer, I felt sure, than Magellan would have taken. We ran into a tropical hurricane that lasted a week, and averaged only four knots for days at a time, the ship rolling so that nothing but sandwiches could be served. But we were going to Hawaii, a comparative paradise, and when, in the middle of the trip, I received a dispatch from the Bureau of Personnel detaching me upon arrival and directing me to report for reassignment as an LST skipper, my state of mind left little to be desired.

Ellis was not much in evidence during the trip. The convoy commodore, a tall, ascetic-looking man, and a Regular Navy commander, was on our ship, and Ellis had not only to vacate his big cabin, hiding the floppy dolls and explaining the smell of perfume as the result of an accident to "a little bottle" he was going to send home to his wife, but to act like an officer when the Commander was around. So Ellis spent as much time as he could sulking in a smaller cabin, while I, acting as navigator for the Commander, was almost immune from Ellis's supervision. All the rest of us were, of course, delighted with the Commander's presence and made Ellis feel this as much as we could. Whenever he called me to his cabin, I would glance at my watch and say, "I'm sorry, sir, but the Commander's waiting for me on the bridge," while in the wardroom, even during our rocky sandwich-meals, we sprang to attention when the Commander entered, with a tautness that showed where our admiration lay.

The Commander was a man of extraordinary energy. When not on the bridge, he would sit in his cabin and ask for various ship's reports, which he would check over, more as a diversion, apparently, than as a duty, for he was not our group commander. He would point out errors to Ellis in a dry tone, without at all indicating that he expected them to be corrected. Ellis, having no idea where he stood, became almost hysterical.

"Who does he think he is?" he cried one day when he was

desperate enough to appeal for even my sympathy. "Doesn't he know I'm skipper here? I could confine him to his cabin, and I've half a mind to do it."

I smiled. "And he could relieve you of command."

"Well, let him!" Ellis cried petulantly. "Do you think I wanted to command this Chris-Craft? Do you think I enjoy listening to your Harvard accent?"

"Yale," I again corrected him.

"What's it to me, Yale or Harvard!" he shouted. "A fat lot you learned there. You've got as much loyalty in you as a cat. Loyalty up and loyalty down — you're a fine example, I must say. I know damn well how much loyalty up there is on this ship, and you can bet your last dollar that when it comes to loyalty down — "

I looked at my watch.

"I'm speaking to you!" he almost screamed.

"I'm sorry, sir. The Commander has asked me to speak to him about the noon position."

"Oh, get out of here! Get the hell out!" I was turning to go when he bawled at me, "No! Come back here!"

"Yes, sir?"

"You think you're the only man on board qualified to run this ship, don't you?"

I said nothing.

"Don't you?" he repeated.

"No, sir. I think the Commander is qualified."

Ellis almost choked. After he regained his self-control, he said, "Let me tell you something. You're leaving us in Pearl. Fine. I won't pretend I'm sorry. Until then, you're still the navigator. But Mr. Horner will be the new exec when you're detached, and I'm making him exec as of *now*. You needn't complain to your precious Commander, either. I'll tell him I'm doing it to break Horner in. Is that clear? You can navigate and only navigate. I don't want you on the conning tower. I don't want you in the ship's office. I don't want you to relieve the officer of the deck. Get it? Make your reports to the O.O.D. and stay out of my way! That's all I ask!"

I nodded. If this arrangement suited him, it suited me even better. "Aye aye, sir," I said, and went back up to the bridge.

On the last part of our voyage, as we approached our destination, the sea was level and calm. At 0530 on the morning of our arrival, I was standing with the chief quartermaster on the port wing of the navigator's bridge, watching, through binoculars, a small object in the water — the sea buoy marking the approach to Pearl Harbor. We had picked it up earlier, and the Captain and the Commander had come up on the bridge to change the convoy course accordingly. Now they had gone below again, and I could enjoy the early morning mist, Diamond Head shaping up in the distance, and the foam dancing along the side of what seemed, after our slow progress, a swiftly moving ship.

The chief quartermaster was taking bearings on the buoy. He was a silent, able, almost overconscientious man, to whom I always deferred in navigational questions. Although he never said it, I knew that his sympathies were more with me than with Ellis. I think he must have regarded the Captain, who, as I've said, was a former chief himself, as a blot on the rating.

"There's a fair set here, Mr. W.," he pointed out. "We're being carried down on the buoy."

I went over and took a couple of bearings. "You think five degrees to the right?" I asked.

"Ten ought to do it."

I walked into the wheelhouse and shouted up the voice tube to the officer of the deck. "Mr. Beers!"

"Aye aye, sir."

Mr. Beers was a cheerful, well-meaning ensign who always said "Aye aye" when he should have said "Yes."

"There seems to be quite a set. I suggest you steer ten degrees to the right to maintain course."

"I've noticed the set, Mr. W. I think the present course will clear the buoy."

The chief and I looked at each other in surprise. There was almost a titter from the men in the wheelhouse.

"Okay, she's your baby," I said into the tube.

I have spoken a good deal about the Captain's unpopularity with the other officers and nothing about my own. They preferred me to him, I believe, but at the same time they resented my fussiness. Mr. Beers was obviously making use of the Captain's restriction of my role to navigator. I left the wheelhouse and rejoined the chief.

"Chief," I said, "I want the quartermaster of the watch to report every five minutes to Mr. Beers my advice as to changing course. See that he logs it, too."

"Aye aye, sir."

I stared at the buoy through my binoculars. The chief came back after speaking to the quartermaster and started taking bearings again.

"He's going to smack it all right, sir."

"Oh, no, Chief. That would be awful."

We exchanged a long, understanding look.

"Awful, sir."

I glanced up at Mr. Beers on the conning tower. I could see that he, too, was staring at the buoy. He was worried himself now, but, happily for me, he was hardheaded.

"You know, sir," the chief said to me after taking another bearing, "he might just miss it."

"Please, Chief! Don't even think it."

The buoy was coming rapidly closer now, and the bearings were not changing. I watched it, fascinated. It was like a magnet, drawing the ship nearer and nearer.

"Recommend fifteen degrees to the right!" I shouted up. "Twenty!"

Mr. Beers was at last alive to what was happening. The buoy was almost upon us. He vigorously put on right rudder, but the buoy and the ship were now destined for each other as unalterably as Captain Ahab and his whale, and the chief and I, jumping up and down with excitement, leaned over the rail and yelled like schoolboys as the buoy struck a third of the way down the portside and ducked under the ship. We could hear it pounding along the bottom — a wonderful booming sound — and I ran into the radar room. On the radar screen, I saw the buoy reappear suddenly behind us, a small dot behind a larger one, and then I saw it disappear again under the next large dot. The second ship in the convoy had gone over it. And then the third —

Through the tube now, I could hear Ellis's voice. He

was already on the conning tower. "Come up here, Mr. W."

When I went up, he was still shouting at the crestfallen Mr. Beers. He spun around to me immediately.

"Did you tell him about the set?"

"Every five minutes for thirty minutes, sir. It's in the log."

"Why didn't you relieve him?"

"Your orders, sir."

He looked past me with sudden fear in his eyes. I turned and saw the Commander's figure looming in the doorway to the conning tower.

"For Christ's sake, Ellis, this is the sorriest job I've ever seen!" he roared. "If you can't bring a ship into Pearl on a flat sea without running over a buoy, you ought to go back to chief! Now, don't give me any excuses. I don't want any excuses."

I stood there and listened to Ellis's humiliation. It almost made up to me for a year of petty persecution, and when it was over, I was sated. I was more than sated; I was ashamed. It occurred to me for the first time what the buoy might have done to the screws of the ships that went over it. It was to this that our bickering had reduced me, who had made such an issue of Ellis's failure to co-operate in fighting the war. When I returned to the port wing of the navigator's bridge and leaned against the rail to watch the approaching shoreline, I reached in my pocket and heard the consoling crackle of the dispatch slip on which my orders for reassignment had been typed.

THE LEGENDS OF
HENRY EVERETT

THE LEGENDS OF HENRY EVERETT

WHEN I FIRST WENT TO WORK AS A CLERK FOR THE law firm of Everett & Coates, Henry Fellows Everett was already more of a legend than a man. He was in his early eighties and one of the last of that great generation of lawyers, the generation of Paul D. Cravath and Francis Lynde Stetson, which had forged the modern corporate law firm, that bright and gleaming sword, out of the rusty materials lying about the old-fashioned city lawyer's office of seventy years ago. The members of these firms today, and indeed for the past thirty years, have unlike their predecessors conformed to a certain pattern: they have become genial, available, democratic with their clerks and sympathetic with their clients, ready with a generality for every emergency and a funny story for every banquet. Eccentricity, the prerogative of the older generation, has gone out of fashion, though the middle-aged lawyer still remembers it lovingly and tells nostalgic tales of his early clerkship when he was shouted at and abused by a ferocious but magnificent taskmaster. This nostalgia, of course, is not so much a nostalgia for the days of his own subordination as for the era of the lawyer's greater glory, that halcyon time when clients as well as clerks could be shouted at, even shown the door, when fees were paid in the stock of expanding companies, when a Joseph H. Choate could persuade the Supreme Court that an income tax was unconstitutional and a William Nelson Cromwell could negotiate the Panama Canal.

Mr. Everett, younger than any of these individuals and correspondingly less of an individualist, was nonetheless a true member of the great generation. His paneled office in Everett & Coates, twice as large as any other, was hung with photographs of statesmen and peace conferences and framed illuminated manuscripts expressing tribute and conferring degrees. Rarely if ever did a clerk penetrate its interior; Mr. Everett dealt almost exclusively with his partners, who addressed him as "Chief" with a little smile that only heightened one's sense of their veneration. He was a small thin man with stooping shoulders and long, thin, brown sunken cheeks. He had gray hair, parted in the middle, which always sat so neatly on the top of his head that I think it must have been a toupee. He had large clear eyes that were almost expressionless and a sharp, rasping voice except when he spoke in public, when it had the emotional mellifluousness that comes with self-confidence or even self-admiration. He was direct, nervous and highly irritable; he was always, so to speak, stripped for action, and his single-mindedness made one feel disorganized and inefficient. It was not till I saw him one day wearing a golf cap, a bow tie and a pair of knickers that it struck me of a sudden that his air of intensity and preoccupation was that of a small boy.

The first time that I worked for Mr. Everett directly

was when I went up to his house on Madison Avenue to take him and Mrs. Everett their wills. They were leaving for Europe that night and the will signing, as was always the case with his personal affairs, had been put off by the old man to the last moment, when there was no one but myself in the department to handle it. The other clerk, whom I had brought to act as a witness, and I were ushered into the library to wait. Law reports lined the high shelves; the portrait of Mr. Everett over the mantel, in the robes of a Harvard doctor of laws, stared through open mahogany doors at the brooding marble figure of Justice in the hall. The atmosphere was dank, institutional, more like a bar association than a private house.

When Mr. Everett appeared he was, as usual, nervous and impatient. He barely nodded to us.

"Have you got it there?" he snapped, taking the will from me. "Lot of damn foolishness this doing a will over every year." He sat down and turned the pages quickly, muttering to himself as he did so. "Trying to take advantage of every last wrinkle in the new tax laws. Trying too hard, that's what I tell them."

Mrs. Everett came in and shook hands with us, very nicely. She was a plain, dumpy woman with a round face and dyed red hair. She was bigger than her husband and seemed to be trying to contract herself to a more suitable size. I had heard that she behaved more like a trained nurse to her husband than a wife, giving in to him in everything except his health, but supervising that to an alarming degree, calling up his office and canceling his appointments without warning, hiding his briefcase, changing travel accommodations, and bearing the angry storm of his resentment with the glittering little smile of the dedicated. She settled down at a table with her will, putting on her pince-nez.

"I won't understand a word of it, you know," she complained timidly to me. "I never do. Do I really have to read it?"

"I'm afraid you should."

"Mrs. Everett read the copy you sent her," her husband snapped at me impatiently. "She and I went over it together and approved it. This is the same thing, isn't it?"

"Yes, sir. But how can she be sure unless she reads the original?"

"Oh, bother, Westcott," the old man retorted, "she knows what she wants done, and this does it. You can't expect her to follow the jargon. I've been over it myself, clause by clause, with Kingman."

I swallowed hard. Mr. Kingman, my boss, had specifically instructed me to be sure that they both read the originals.

"Let me put it this way, sir," I said. "Suppose there were ever a question and I had to testify? Wouldn't I have to say under oath that Mrs. Everett not only wouldn't read her will, but that she hadn't understood it?"

For a moment he glared at me and then grunted and looked away.

"All right, all right," he said. "If we must go through the rigmarole, I suppose we must. I'll run over it again with her."

He leaned over Mrs. Everett's shoulder and started

explaining the will to her, summarizing the provisions hastily and inaccurately and turning the pages with an impatient hand while she sat beneath him, quiet and uncomprehending. I said nothing. I had exhausted my courage.

"All right," he said at last, handing the wills back to me. "What next? Can we actually sign them? Or do you have some other hocus-pocus?"

He made an even worse fuss when I insisted on asking him the proper questions: whether or not he had read his will, whether it had been prepared in accordance with his instructions, whether we were to act as witnesses, and so forth. He finally raised both his hands above his head in a mock gesture of oath-taking and snapped: "Yes, yes, yes, I swear, so help me, amen, whatever you want, but let's get on with it, for heaven's sake," and taking the document from my hand he signed his name on the last page with a great sprawling flourish. It was only when I picked it up to read the attestation clause that I saw that he had signed Mrs. Everett's will. I looked around at the other witness, who was peering over my shoulder. His eyes were round with dismay.

"Mr. Everett," I said falteringly.

"Yes, yes, what is it?"

"You've signed your wife's will."

"What's that? Give it here." He snatched it from me again and stared at it soberly. "Well, my God! Why in the name of thunder don't they send somebody who knows enough to give me the right will?" He turned on me, his eyes bright. "Or would that be asking too much? I suppose it would. I suppose, in this day and age, it really would!"

"I didn't give it to you, sir," I said sullenly. "You took it from me. And if I may say so, this whole thing has been too hurried from the start."

He stared at me for a moment, and then back at the inappropriate signature.

"Mrs. Everett can scratch it out," he said in a milder tone, "and then sign her own name under it. The presence of my signature is, after all, legally speaking, an irrelevance."

"That may be true, sir," I said, feeling bolder as he seemed to back down. "But it would be foolish, in my opinion, to take any chances. I'll have the will retyped and bring it back tonight."

"But I'm sailing for Europe tonight!"

"Then I'll bring it to the boat."

He gave me a sharp look.

"Are you working on the theory," he demanded, "that I'm one of those old fools who likes to be barked back at? Because I warn you, I find that theory a most offensive one. For years now impertinent young men from the office have invaded the privacy of my home to holler at me. It has not got them ahead, I assure you."

"I'm not hollering, Mr. Everett," I pointed out. "I'm only telling you the things that I'm supposed to tell you."

After the pause that followed this, he simply nodded.

"I'll see you at the boat," he said.

Apparently however, he did not mind occasional firm treatment, for when I went that night with my other witness to his cabin on the *Queen Mary* he signed his will as docilely as an office stenographer getting her legal work free.

He then made us stay while he and Mrs. Everett entertained the partners and their wives who had come to see them off. He proved a surprisingly genial host, moving jerkily around the stateroom to see that everyone had enough champagne, laughing loudly if rather mirthlessly at their jokes and telling legal anecdotes and even fishing stories. I had a curious feeling, however, that he was playing a role and enjoying it, as he must have enjoyed playing the old tartar that afternoon.

I didn't work for him again until some weeks after his return from Europe when I was delegated, in Mr. Kingman's absence, to accompany him to the Appellate Division where he was to argue a will contest on appeal. It was really not a case of sufficient importance to warrant his time, but the decedent had been a friend of his, and he had insisted on handling it personally. I was glad of the chance to see the great man at work. He spoke easily and smoothly before five judges, all of whom knew and respected him and none of whom, I imagined, would have pressed him too closely with tight questions. It was more like a legal discussion over an after-dinner brandy than an argument in court, and I felt rather sorry for the plaintiff's lawyer, to whom Mr. Everett showed the good manners of a clubman to a fellow member's guest who is misbehaving himself.

I congratulated him afterward, as we got into the back

of his car, and he chuckled, obviously pleased.

"Experience still counts for something, Westcott," he said, leaning back in his seat. "Not much, I grant, but something. Oh, yes, still something."

He was in a good mood and insisted on taking me up-town to his club for a drink. I murmured something about going back to the office, which he dismissed with a single impatient gesture of his hand. Obviously, he wanted to talk.

"They say we don't have the judges we used to have," he told me gruffly as we sat at a table in the dark, empty bar, each with a dry martini. "Don't believe a word of it. Take those fellows this afternoon. Good men, every one of them. Of course, everything in the past seems better when you're middle-aged. But when you're old the way I am, it all seems part of the same thing. And the past doesn't impress you any more than the present, or the future, for that matter. The sacred Holmes, for example. They worship him today. I always thought he was a bit of a charlatan myself, with his endless chatter about manhood and war. Did you ever read a speech of his called 'The Soldier's Faith'? 'I thank God for our polo players,' he says. And why? Because they risk life and limb." He snorted contemptuously. "That's Holmes to the life. Afraid we'd go soft unless we might get killed."

"You mean he was like Hemingway?" I asked. "A muscular philosopher?"

He fixed me with his blank stare, a reminder, perhaps, that I was there to listen, not to comment.

"I haven't read your Mr. Hemingway," he retorted.

"I haven't read his fiction, that is. But then I don't read fiction. I read poetry, philosophy and history, and I counsel you to do the same. Oh, I've read his *Death in the Afternoon,* yes." He nodded several times at this. "But that, after all, is different. That deals with my favorite subject."

I stared.

"Do you mean bullfighting, sir?"

He laughed. It was a harsh, jarring laugh.

"I mean death, young man," he said emphatically. Then he looked at me for a moment with a gaze that seemed to be taking in things behind me. "Oh, you're uncomfortable now, of course," he continued in a remote, sarcastic tone. "The old, I know, should never mention death. It's so far from you and so near to us. But what do you think we *think* about, we old?"

I lowered my eyes in embarrassment.

"We think about all the things you hope you won't be thinking about when *you're* old," he went on bitterly. "We think about when we're going to die, and what happens to us then. And don't let anybody fool you, young man, we think about it all the time!"

"You don't believe in an after-life, sir?"

My question rang out, hollow and fatuous, and I waited for him to jump down my throat. But he only shrugged his shoulders.

"Oh, I used to," he said, suddenly tired. "When I was young. I had faith in a scared, self-deluding sort of way. But my older brother was an atheist. It used to make him angry that I would never *know* that he was right and I was wrong. He said there ought to be a moment after death when the truth was made known. Just a single, clear, all-knowing moment before eternal blackness. And in that moment, he used to say, I would hear him laughing. Like Alberich in the darkness."

"How horrible!"

My exclamation broke into his mood and seemed to change it.

"It was horrible, wasn't it?" he said in a milder tone, smiling again. "Well, who knows? Perhaps I shall hear him. Perhaps not. But you need another drink. And, by the way, I should like you to dine with Mrs. Everett and myself tonight. It will be dull for you, but it will be a change for us. And the old should have some prerogatives."

I assured him that it would not be dull for me, but he only shrugged his shoulders again. It was obviously a matter of indifference to him whether or not it was. We had another drink and motored up to his house.

We were five at dinner, as the Edward Everetts as well as myself had been invited. Edward was Mr. Everett's only son, about fifty, thin and bald and tired-looking. A partner in Everett & Coates, a position which he owed quite as much to his own ability as to his father's, he was a dry, harmless man of superficial friendliness who laughed pleasantly enough at other people's jokes and rarely told any of his own. It was his own way, perhaps, of indicating his belief that no subject other than law could really be taken seriously. His wife was a tense, rather gasping woman who kept her sharp black eyes riveted on her father-in-law during dinner, exclaiming over each truculent monosyllable that he dropped.

"I wish I'd heard you in court today, Papa," she cried. "I bet you were simply scrumptious! Wasn't he scrumptious, Mr. Westcott?"

"I suppose you might call it that, Mrs. Everett."

"Suppose? Aren't you *sure?*"

"Perhaps, Helen, Mr. Westcott would have used another word to describe me. He has sharp eyes, and youth, you know, can be cruel."

"Not to you, darling. *Never!*"

The old man turned away from her.

"Did you get a chance to read my brief, Edward? Do you think they'll reverse?"

"Of course, I don't know, Father, if the Appellate Division decides cases on the basis of scrumptiousness — "

"Edward, you're making fun of me? Before your father, too!"

"Not at all, my dear. But to answer your question, Father, I would think, in the light of Bryan versus Fox — "

"Oh, Edward, of course, your father will win! Arguing the case himself and all that! Won't he, Mother Everett?"

"He's not going to win anything at all if he keeps up this pace. Henry, you're to go to bed at nine o'clock tonight. Remember you promised me?"

I sat in growing indignation during the rest of the meal as Mrs. Edward cooed at the old man, patted his hand, shrieked hysterically if he said anything that could be construed as funny, keeping him amused, for all the world as if he had come down for the weekend from a sanatorium, while his wife, silent, thinking only of the meal, not listening to the conversation, frowned at the butler and wagged a warning finger to indicate "no more fruit for Mr.

Everett" or no more wine for his already empty glass.

It was, I could immediately see, the other side of the coin, the domestic version of the downtown legend. If in the office Mr. Everett was renowned as a tartar, a disciplinarian, a man who made other men jump, in the home this picture was to be softened by the touch of the old "sweetie-pie," the husband who meekly puts on his rubbers when his wife directs, the family man, to be loved, bullied, cajoled and passionately defended against all who might "misunderstand" him.

He seemed to have a sense of this himself, for after dinner he took me down to the library alone, leaving the others in the living room.

"There's something I want to discuss with you, Westcott," he said, sitting by the fire and stretching out his feet on the footstool. "I have a speech to make to the bar association on the sixtieth anniversary of my admission to the bar. It occurred to me that you might be of some assistance. Ordinarily I work these things out with somebody at the office with more experience than you have, but I think you and I might find our points of view congenial." I told him I would be flattered.

"What will your speech be about, sir?"

"What do you think?" he demanded, turning suddenly and fixing me with a stare of mock indignation. "What do you ever hear on such occasions? There's a recognized pattern, isn't there? I shall begin with the customary recollections of the great departed professors of law at Harvard. I will then proceed to a series of heart-warming anecdotes about my early practice. One of these will deal with a rusty old judge, some famous, lovable character of the period. It will, also, of course, serve to illustrate the intensity of my early industry in contrast to the relaxed standards of today. After this it will be almost time for me to spread my wings and flap off into the blue skies of legal philosophy, quoting Plato, Cardozo and Holmes, reasserting my faith in mankind and the bar despite the threat of communism and the atom bomb. And I shall conclude, needless to say, with a ringing note of hope for the future." Here he jumped to his feet and stretched out his arms like a dramatic orator. " 'And as the curtain descends for the last time upon my life, as surely as it appears, but only appears, to descend upon our free world today, I can yet see, in the glimmer of lights along the bay — ' " He broke off with a snort. "You finish it. Any way you want. With Arnold or Marshall or Gray. Or even with your favorite Mr. Hemingway, if you choose. For you see what I see, young man. You see it doesn't amount to a hill of beans."

There was a knock at the door, but it opened before Mr. Everett could even grunt, and the round shining eyes and long thin nose of his daughter-in-law poked in at us.

"Are you working, Papa? Are you letting him, Mr. Westcott? Oh, for shame! When we all know he's been in court today and needs his rest. Oh, no. Come upstairs, Papa, and trounce me at backgammon. You know, he can, too, Mr. Westcott. You never saw such a fiend at any game."

"I'll be up when I'm ready, Helen," he said sharply. "I'm busy now."

Her face grew very long at this, with a kind of mock

humility, and she winked at me as if to show me how to respond to his changes of mood, how to shift to the role of the hurt and sulking child.

"All right, if that's the way you're going to treat me," she said, with a little pout. "Just you see if I'll stay here another minute. I'll go up and tell Mother Everett on you."

When she had closed the door again, Mr. Everett turned to me with quiet acidity.

"You will excuse my daughter-in-law," he said. "Her apologists tell me that she means well and that she thinks I enjoy being treated like an un-house-trained puppy. Dear me. I remember, some years ago, when I had the good fortune to have Morris Cohen here for dinner. The poor gentleman was obliged for some minutes to carry on a conversation with Helen. I shall never forget his response to one of her questions. 'My dear young lady,' he said, 'how can I answer you? Your remark is without thought content.' Perfect, wasn't it? Without thought content. And such simplicity, too. Classic."

I felt my first, perhaps rather belated chill at this. Helen was a fool, of course, but even I could see that her apologists, whoever they were, might be right. Undoubtedly she did mean well. There had been a coldness in his manner of repeating Mr. Cohen's remark, an absence of family feeling that seemed suddenly to twitch off the poor woman's covering and to expose her, stripped and shivering. It was not a pleasant picture. I wanted to admire Mr. Everett; I was excited and flattered by his notice of me, but when I really admired I hated reservations, and there was a touch of cruelty in his air of satisfaction that I could not ignore. Walking home later that night I decided that if he saw things clearly, heartlessly, even destructively, it was only to a chosen few whose discretion he trusted that he imparted his vision. For the rest he fulfilled his family duties. He submitted for the most part unprotestingly to the loving if misguided ministrations of his relatives. He discussed fishing and even baseball with his partners. He was benign when the situation required. To such a man a lack of charity could occasionally be forgiven. Certainly by his intimates, if one had the honor to be of that small and privileged group. Already, although I did not know it, I was doing what the others had done. I was constructing my own legend of Henry Everett.

When I was again summoned to Mr. Everett's, a week later, I found him alone in the library. He seemed quite pleased about something.

"I know just how we'll do it, Westcott," he exclaimed as I came in, "I see it all. The speech will be in the mood of Tennyson's 'Ulysses,' filled with the note of what may yet be done. 'Tho' much is taken, much abides,' that idea. What do you think?"

I hesitated.

"You think it's corny?"

"I'm afraid I do, sir."

"But they'll love it, you know they will!"

"Yes, sir. I'm afraid they will."

He chuckled and turned back to the book of poetry in his hand.

"I like this bit about Telemachus. It's Edward to the life." He read aloud to me:

> *Most blameless is he, centered in the sphere*
> *Of common duties, decent not to fail*
> *In offices of tenderness, and pay*
> *Meet adoration to my household gods,*
> *When I am gone.*

He nodded his head several times, in agreement with the bard. "And Ulysses has no use for him, that's the point." He put the book down and stared silently into the fire. I could feel his good humor slipping away from him already as it had at his club when we had discussed death. "Which means, of course," he continued with a sigh, "that I have no use for Edward. He's so middle-aged, you see, and we old have no use for middle age. Now he and Helen have a son — you don't know him, he's still in law school — who has that precious glow of youth in his eyes. It will all be gone at twenty-five, I know, and maybe it's just as well. Then he can get on with the serious business of living, and I predict that he will be more fatuous than his mother. But nonetheless, when he turns his wide eyes on me and asks, as if he were the first person in the whole world to have thought of it, 'Grandpa, do you think a lawyer should represent a man whom he knows to be guilty?' I care more than when Edward tells me about the last case he's argued before the Supreme Court. And make no mistake, Edward is a first-class lawyer, which that boy will never be. That's the thing about Edward. He's good."

I watched him silently, knowing by now that he did not pause for my comments.

"And who am I to sneer at Edward?" he went on in sudden anger, getting up and coming toward me menacingly. "An old fool who likes to think he's Ulysses so he can look down at Telemachus! Strutting about and puffing and pretending that at eighty-two he's going 'to sail beyond the sunset, and the baths of all the western stars' until he dies!" He stretched both his arms out in bitter parody of his own self-dramatization. "I'm an ass, Westcott! Remember that, an ass! Yet even as I say it, I'm secretly hoping that you'll still find me magnificent. I'm acting for you as much as I shall be acting for the bar association when I make that speech!"

He collapsed once again into his chair and his head slumped forward on his chest. The room was suddenly full of his stertorous breathing.

I got up in a panic, wondering if he had had a heart attack.

"Mr. Everett!" I cried. "Mr. Everett," I repeated, "are you all right?"

"Go away, young man," he muttered. "Go away."

I hurried upstairs to find Mrs. Everett, who was in the sitting room. She followed me swiftly, without a word, but when we got to the library the heavy breathing had stopped. He was asleep. She examined him sharply for a moment and then nodded, in relief.

"You may as well go now, Mr. Westcott," she whispered. "We'll let you know when he needs you again."

They never did, however, nor was I surprised. It would have been perfectly natural for the family to assume that my effect on the old man was disturbing. This could even, I suppose, have been true, although it seemed unlikely to me. Any other young and respectful person could have served him as well for an audience. A few days later Edward Everett came into my office with the uneasy cordiality of the partner making a personal visit. There was a shy, semiconspiratorial air about him, as though he were trying to let me know that he knew what I had seen and heard and was begging me, timidly enough but nicely enough, to be quiet about it.

"The old man appreciates what you've done, Peter," he said, "and you'll be glad to know that he's got the speech licked. It's just a question of a few finishing touches. He told me to tell you that he thinks he can do the rest alone. I can give him a hand myself if he needs it."

As a matter of fact, I was relieved. I had not been looking forward to my next session with Mr. Everett. It was one thing to play with the idea that I had become, in some curious fashion, the spiritual intimate of the old man's final chapter, that I might, if the relationship continued, find myself at some future date an indispensable witness to his biographers. It was quite another to be the lonely companion of his melancholia. I may have been sufficiently a dissenter to have enjoyed hearing the old and revered idol belch in the solitude of his temple and to have laughed at his sneers at the officious priests who busied themselves about the folds of his garments. But that was enough. When he grasped the pillars of the temple like the blind Samson and threatened to bring down the whole structure on top of all the priests, including even the doubters like myself, it was time to get out. I had to live in this world, and presumably for a longer time in the future than Mr. Everett.

I did not see him again until the bar association dinner was given in the banquet hall of a large hotel and attended by several hundred people, including all the partners and associates of Everett & Coates. The old man, looking very well, sat, of course, at the head table between the president of the association and the chief judge of the Court of Appeals. He listened to the long speeches of praise rendered in his honor with the air of one practiced in that delicate art. He sat with his head hanging down, very still, occasionally shaking it sharply to indicate his failure to merit some particular fulsome tribute. When he laughed at a joke, he laughed heartily, shaking both shoulders. The applause when he finally rose to speak was tumultuous.

"It is commonly said that the wisest man is he who knows that he knows nothing," he began. Then he paused and reached down for his napkin with which he lightly touched his lips.

His voice, as always when he spoke in public, was rich and strong. "I wonder how many of us ever really stop to consider what it means to know nothing. Nothing at all." He paused again for emphasis. "Not even to know, for example, what Descartes assumed: that man is a thinking creature. Not even to know, as an obvious consequence, that he exists at all. Oh, I can assure you, ladies and gentlemen, that when a man really and truly *knows* that he knows nothing, he does not purr about it from behind a white waistcoat to the eminent members of his profession."

There was a ripple of appreciative laughter. Mr. Everett however, kept his eyes dramatically and abstractedly fixed on the wall opposite him. "He locks himself up, rather," he continued grimly, "in the silence of his chamber and has the good grace not to inflict his discovery on young people whose eyes are filled with the warm charm of their own illusion. If he knows anything — that is, if he knows that he has learned nothing — he knows that this illusion is worth all the clairvoyance that ignorant people admire in himself."

I stirred self-consciously in my chair, wondering if these words could possibly be meant for me, if this was his handsome if rather dramatic apology for any bewilderment he might have caused me. I glanced about at my neighbors to see if they noted anything unusual in the speech. Their faces, however, were bland and composed. Most of them, of course, were only half listening, lulled by the roll of after-dinner sentences, expecting what they were used to, nobility of expression, high dignity of thought, a double scotch and soda, and an early evening. Surely, however, some would listen and understand and shudder at the bleak wind of his doubts, surely some would see the consequences of his destructive premise. But I was going, as usual, too far. They would assume, would they not, that he was dealing in paradoxes, that the right arm of the accomplished speaker would gather in all that the left had scattered wide?

And they assumed correctly, for in a minute he went on.

"But it is one thing to know or even suspect that one knows nothing and quite another to *believe* in nothing — "

So there it was, the stratagem, and I could breathe in relief, as he rolled easily on from the terrors of conscious ignorance to the compensations of faith, from Nietzsche and Spengler and nihilism and the ultimate horror of Hitler and Stalin to the principles of Jefferson and the early fathers and their validity today. He gave himself a field day; he was more exuberant, more emotional, more convincing than I would have believed possible, and when he ended with the words of Holmes on his ninetieth birthday, the entire room rose and the applause lasted for ten uninterrupted minutes. If he was acting, as he had told me, I could only conclude that, at least for the moment, he had convinced himself. The tears in his eyes were real. Turning, when it was all over, to take my place in the long, slow line of men before the coat closet, I saw Mrs. Edward give her husband a timid little smile of congratulation across the table where we had been sitting.

THE GREAT WORLD
AND
TIMOTHY COLT

Timothy Colt, when I first met him, was the most promising law clerk in Everett & Coates. He was then thirty-three, four years older than myself, with one foot already poised to take the final step to partnership, that goal to which our energies were consecrated and which would remove him forever from the bare, cream-painted rooms of the associates, hung with *Vanity Fair* cartoons of British judges and solicitors, to the paneled offices, albeit at first the smallest, of the members of the firm. He had the rather haggard, if handsome, looks of the overworked young man who is not, however, working in vain; his face was thin, pale and cerebral, his eyes large and dark, with an appraising, noncommittal, faintly amused look. His hair was thick and shiningly black, and he had a habit of tugging at it that kept it boyishly out of place. There were moments, indeed, when he reminded me of a romantic portrait of the early last century, fragile and wide-eyed, bent over a book in a Gothic study, the fingertips of one hand resting on the head of a devoted retriever, but it was an impression soon dispelled by his own wholly sincere unawareness that his looks were any but those of a typical downtown law clerk. He had come into the firm originally under the auspices of Mr. Hazard, for whose four small daughters he had once been a summer tutor.

"It was after my second year at Columbia law," Timmy told me once, "and I really was dog-tired. But I had to have the money, and at least it was outdoors work, tennis and riding, things like that. And then Hazard discovered I'd written a note for the law review on a case he'd argued in the Appellate Division. Jesus!" He shook his head. "That really did it. We worked on a new brief for the Court of Appeals all of August, and another tutor had to be sent up for the girls. It damn near killed me, but it was worth it. It cinched me a job in Everett & Coates."

It was like Timmy to assume that he was more indebted to the chance interest of a senior partner than to his own capabilities. I knew otherwise, after six months as his principal assistant. We worked at least four nights a week and all of Saturday, and before we were through my social life had virtually ceased to exist. The outer world, in fact, had fallen away so completely that its infrequent manifestations, the letters in my mailbox at night, the occasional telegram with a holiday greeting, seemed oddly irrelevant, and I was perfectly happy of a Saturday evening simply to go to the Colts' and discuss with them over many drinks what Timmy and I had been doing all week. Of course, it was shop talk, shop talk with a vengeance, but somehow there didn't seem much point in discussing the books we hadn't had time to read or the people we hadn't seen. Fortunately for Flora Colt, she, too, had gone to law school.

"I sat next to Timmy in every class our first year," she explained to me on one such evening. "My name, you see, was Coleman, which came just before Colt. I used to think what a waste of time it was for people like me to be studying law when people like him were. I guess the only reason I lasted as long as I did was that I was afraid of losing hold of him if I busted out!"

She was certainly the perfect wife for Timmy, utterly content with the restricted life that his late hours imposed. She ran her apartment and took care of her two small noisy boys with an air of rather amiable inefficiency, filling in her spare time, when there was any, with eclectic if rather indiscriminate reading, with crosswords and double acrostics, even with radio serials. Flora could read Mauriac and *Screen Romances* almost simultaneously and, I sometimes suspected, with equal satisfaction. However late Timmy's key turned in the lock, she was never more than barely ready for him, but when she saw him and smiled, with the smile that made up so fully for her large, over-serious features, her undisciplined blond hair, her constant habit of wearing brown, the evening was all his. The other things, the books, the radio, even the little boys were firmly if affectionately relegated to second place. Flora's heart was so big that it was hard to believe as one did believe, that Timmy could occupy all of it.

On one of those Saturday nights at Timmy's, with just the three of us present, he was holding forth on the virtues of Sam Liendecker, a new client whom I had not met.

"Liendecker, Liendecker!" Flora interrupted. "All I hear now is Liendecker! I sometimes wonder," she con-

tinued, turning to me, "if I wouldn't rather lose Timmy
to a blonde."

"Mr. Liendecker is a very able man, darling," Timmy reminded her. "He got American Export and Canning out
of the red in five years' time. Their common was selling
at ten when he took over, and it's now quoted at one thirty-
five. Which I think even you will admit, Flora, is grounds
for admiration."

I couldn't help glancing at the hole in the arm of the sofa
that had been burned by a cigarette three months before.
Or at one of the boys' trolleys under the sideboard that
had been there the preceding week and would certainly
be there the next. I was sure Timmy never noticed such
things.

"Why do you admire success so, Timmy?" I asked him.

"Don't we all?"

"Not the way you do. No matter what sort of an ogre
a man may be, you always think you can shut me and
Flora up by pointing out that he's a success."

Timmy laughed quickly, rather too quickly as he was apt
to when conversation became personal.

"Isn't that what's made this country great?"

"Is it? And, anyway, what of it?"

"Well, of course, Peter, if you're just going to say 'What
of it' to everything — " he was beginning.

"You don't see what I mean," I interrupted. "If a thing
is there, it's there. We accept it. But I thought we only
admired what we wanted ourselves. What do successful
men have that you want?"

"Why, he wants what everyone else wants," Flora intervened, "a bigger car and a bigger apartment —"

"But he doesn't," I protested, turning around to her, "that's just the point. And what do *you* get out of all his work, Flora? Do you have a mink coat? Or a house by the seashore? Or even a country club? Good God, woman, what do you live for?"

Flora's sense of humor, never the keenest, would desert her altogether after three drinks.

"Now just a minute, Peter Westcott," she said pointing her finger at me, "it's going to take time before Timmy's in a position to buy me those things. But that's not the point. The point is, he gives me everything I want, right now. Everything in the world!"

"Everything?" I queried. "No nurse? No private school for the boys?"

"Timmy and I went to public school here in New York!" Flora exclaimed indignantly, moving over to her husband and putting her arm around his shoulders. "And we don't happen to feel that either of our boys is going to faint away if he finds himself sitting next to a colored child!"

Timmy joined in my happy burst of laughter.

"Flora, darling," he said, patting the hand that was on his shoulder, "he's only kidding you."

"Well, I don't like that kind of kidding."

"But I'm not criticizing, Flora," I pointed out. "I think it's fine to be like you and Timmy. Never keeping up with the Joneses. Not even bothering to move out of this housing development. Which you could certainly afford to do now."

"Could we?" Timmy looked at his wife and smiled.

"What *do* you do with the money, darling?"

"But if all you want," I continued, "is to be a slave at the office while Flora looks at television — "

"Television!" she exclaimed. "I wish *you* had two children to take care of, Peter!"

"What," I finished imperturbably, "can the great world offer you as a prize?"

"Does it never occur to you, Peter," Timmy demanded, "that the satisfaction of a job well done might be a sufficient reward in itself?"

Well, it might have been for him. I didn't know. But I did know what a different person he was in the office. The moment he crossed the reception hall of Everett & Coates his face assumed a grave, sometimes almost a grim expression. This was where one worked, and to confuse, even briefly, the place where one worked and the place where one played would obviously not do. None of the younger men ever dropped into Timmy's office during the day to smoke a cigarette or to gossip; he would listen politely enough to anyone who did so, for he was always polite, but his nervous, abstracted glances at the papers on his desk soon showed his visitor how little the intrusion was appreciated. At the time of our talk about success he was busier than ever before, working on the purchase by American Export & Canning of a new plant in New Jersey. It was an important deal, yet no partner had been assigned to it, and the rumor had already got around the office that it was to be Timmy's big test. Certainly I had never seen him set so stiff a pace; I was like a mountain climber lashed by a rope to my leader and uncomfortably picking my way after him as he kept disappearing into the mists above. It didn't occur to me that there was anyone else ahead of him in those regions of thin air whom he in turn might be following until one morning in his office I found him talking to a tall thin man who raised a pair of appraising eyes to examine me.

"Oh, Peter," Timmy said immediately, "this is Mr. Liendecker." He turned to the client. "Peter Westcott, sir, who is also working on the deal."

"Westcott," Mr. Liendecker repeated with a brief nod in my direction, as I sat down in the remaining chair. He made no move to shake hands, but, turning back to Timmy, simply resumed the conversation that I had interrupted. I noted with interest his long, angular, pale pink face and smooth, light gray hair. His lips were dry and almost flesh-colored; they bore a determination that might have been half stubbornness, half pride. He was dressed in the gray which, like his eyes and hair, seemed his motif, with expensive brown suede shoes and a pink shirt. But what I couldn't take my eyes off was his tie. It was a silk tie, covered with blue and green bubbles that apparently represented the sea, for between them, in brilliant purple, were woven various manifestations of marine life, here a fin, there a tail, now even a pair of shark-like jaws, all leading the eye down from the green knot to the coiled sea monster which crouched at the wide lower section. It was not that the tie was exactly ugly; it might have been sufficiently startling as a modern chintz. It was simply that as a tie it seemed somehow defiant. It defied Timmy; it defied me; it defied even Everett & Coates and the very view of New York harbor from Timmy's window. As Mr. Liendecker sat back in his chair with the rather ominous immobility of the highly strung, I felt in his eyes and fingers, when he allowed himself to touch that tie, not only a taking it for granted that anyone who could, would buy such a tie, but a challenge, faintly sneering, to any contrary-minded to tell him, Sam Liendecker, why.

"It's not as if I was asking for the final contract," he was saying in a flat voice. "It's only a draft that I want. Why can't you let me have a draft to show these people over the weekend?"

"Because once they've seen a draft, they'll never let us add anything to it," Timmy explained patiently. "We'll show it to them on Monday, sir, and that's a week earlier than they expected it."

"But what's holding it up now?"

"I believe Peter's making a final check," Timmy replied, looking up at me, "on whether or not the executors need a court order before selling the plant."

Mr. Liendecker turned on me.

"Do they?"

"Well — if the will had contained the usual powers of sale — " I was beginning, startled.

"No, no," he interrupted roughly. "Don't give me that legal double talk. I want an opinion. If an executor doesn't have the power to sell a dead man's property, what *does* he have the power to do?"

"Well, he undoubtedly has the power, but if — "

"There! I thought so!"

He turned back to Timmy triumphantly. The latter,

expressionless, stared down for a few moments at the blotter on his desk.

"I know all the probabilities, sir," he said quietly, without looking up. "I know perfectly well that an executor ordinarily has that power. But there are special circumstances here. Maybe I'm being overcareful, but you pay us for care. If I give it up to you now, sir, it won't be right. I can't take the responsibility."

"I see," said Mr. Liendecker, spreading his thin hands over the arms of his chair and half closing his eyes. "But is there really any reason why you *should* take such a responsibility? Isn't that a question for a member of the firm? For Hazard himself, for example?"

Timmy flushed and looked down at his desk.

"Possibly so. You can, of course, see Mr. Hazard any time you choose."

"Naturally," Mr. Liendecker retorted, opening his eyes with a snap. "He's my lawyer, isn't he? What I want to know is whether *you* don't feel that you could profit by his advice in this matter. Whether *you* don't want to consult him?"

Timmy passed his hand over his mouth and looked across the room at me without seeming to take me in.

"I'm doing my best, sir," he said.

"You feel entirely adequate, then, to the situation?"

"I hope so."

"Then we're all set," Mr. Liendecker said, looking at me with a bland, sarcastic half smile. "That's all I wanted to find out." He rose at this and sauntered out, carelessly picking his hat from Timmy's out-basket as he passed. I looked at Timmy for a moment, but he avoided my glance.

"Well, I'll be damned!" I exclaimed. "What's eating him?"

"He's only miffed that he doesn't have a partner on the deal," Timmy explained, almost apologetically. "I can't blame him, really. I'd feel the same way with six million bucks at stake."

"Oh, you would! Well, it so happens that you're better than any partner on this kind of deal. Anyone around here could tell him that."

"Peter," Timmy protested with a sigh, "we've got a job to do. Must we worry about the personality of the client?"

"Can't I even express an opinion? To you?"

"You don't know Liendecker, Peter. He's a man who's come up the hard way. When he took over American Export — "

"Oh, I know all that," I interrupted roughly. "When Hitler took over Germany things were in tough shape."

"Sam Liendecker is hardly a Hitler, Peter," Timmy said mildly.

"That's because you see him from the point of view of a storm trooper," I retorted. "*I* see him from the point of view of the concentration camp!"

As our work went into the drafting stage and I spent more time in Timmy's office, I became even more acutely aware of Mr. Liendecker's personality. He was one of those quiet, motionless men whose presence is as powerful as a strong scent. He would drop in at any time in the morning or afternoon and sit in the armchair, quietly smoking his gold-tipped cigarettes and reading over any documents that happened to be on Timmy's desk. He expected us to go on with our work and ignore him except when he asked questions which he would throw out, always with the same faint note of surprise, his eyes on the paper he was reading, questions that, no matter how many of us happened to be in the room, were always answered, and evidently intended to be answered, by Timmy alone. The latter's response, however disagreeable the question, however many times it had been asked before, was invariably slow, patient and exact. If he ever wanted to raise his voice or slam the door behind Mr. Liendecker's retreating back, he never gave in to the impulse. His conduct, so far as I could see, was perfect, exasperatingly perfect.

Mr. Liendecker, oddly enough, did not extend his obvious hostility to Timmy to the rest of us. He showed toward me, for example, a rather surly geniality and addressed me, when he was in one of his better moods, as "Sonny." Once he even took me out to lunch and questioned me about the office's attitude toward Timmy. At his club, high above the Hudson in an alcove of glass, he might have been showing me the kingdoms of the earth.

"Everyone thinks Timmy's doing a bang-up job," I said stoutly. "Don't you agree?"

"He's got a few things to learn," Mr. Liendecker answered coolly. "What gets a man ahead in this world is knowing how people tick and what they want. You don't learn that by holing yourself up in a two-by-four office and changing commas into semicolons."

"But Timmy's not supposed to deal with people," I pointed out. "He's supposed to draft the papers."

Mr. Liendecker grunted.

"He's supposed to deal with me, isn't he?"

I had no answer to a remark so extraordinary, but it helped me to understand how difficult a problem Timmy was up against. For what Liendecker apparently resented was the intrusion into his field of anything that he couldn't handle himself, the law, in this instance, with its requirement of papers and precautions. He should have been offered the services of a senior partner whose eminence might have done something to allay his own sense of inferiority. This way it was hopeless. There was no means except by flattery to handle the chip on Liendecker's shoulder, and the very view that he took of Timmy precluded recourse to that.

"I don't think he'll find you hard to deal with, sir," I said, "if you'll only give him half a chance."

If I had hoped, after this, that relations between Timmy and his suspicious client would be improved, I was soon disillusioned. Two days later we were summoned to Mr. Hazard's office for a progress report on the American Export deal, and as we traversed the wide corridor past the black framed photographs of long deceased partners, Timmy shook his head gloomily.

"It's bad news," he said. "It's always bad news when Hazard's secretary makes the call."

Henry Knox Hazard, now that Mr. Coates was dead and Mr. Everett so old, was the managing partner of the firm.

He was the gentleman who told you if you got your raise each new year, calling in the asssociates one by one to do so, with a brief congratulatory nod of his head and the flash of a grin that had more charm than you thought it was going to. He was a big, rather magnificent man with a tremendous head and shoulders towering over a body that tapered gradually down, under richly heavy and aristocratically unpressed tweeds, to a pair of long thin legs and formidably shined shoes. He listened now to Timmy with many head noddings, his eyes fixed on the thin ankle that was resting on one knee. When he picked a cigarette out of his vest pocket, Timmy, without pausing in what he had to say, without seeming even to have noticed, casually snapped his lighter and reached it over. The gesture, simple as it was, was somehow expressive of their mutual confidence.

"I see, I see," Mr Hazard said when Timmy had finished. "It looks as if we ought to close on schedule, doesn't it? Good. There's only one thing more." He paused, but as one pauses who has planned to isolate and emphasize his final point. "Sam Liendecker dropped in yesterday. He seems to have an idea that he's not getting the service he wants. What are you doing, Timmy? Doping off?"

I glanced at Timmy, but there was no sign of a smile on his suddenly flushed face.

"Was that his expression, sir?" he asked. "Doping off?"

"It was certainly his implication."

"If you'll look at the time sheets," Timmy said in a choked voice, "I think they'll reassure you. Peter and I went home at three o'clock this morning."

Mr. Hazard simply nodded and then opened a blue-print on his desk. He spread it carefully over his blotter, smoothing down the corners.

"He's been having your real estate descriptions checked at American Export. Here, for example." He tapped the blueprint with his paper cutter. "He claims that this sliver, two hundred square feet, is missing from the pro-posed deed."

Timmy stood motionless for a moment before leaning over the desk. Then, without a word and ignoring Mr. Hazard, he handed me the deed.

"Read from there," he said, pointing to a paragraph. When I had finished he looked up and shook his head several times. Mr. Hazard smiled.

"How about it, Timmy? Is Liendecker right?"

"Apparently, sir. It looks like a hack."

"Then I take it you *have* been doping off?"

There was a heavy pause.

"Yes, sir," Timmy said in a barely audible tone. "It looks as if I'd been doping off."

Mr. Hazard threw back his head and uttered a deep, gravelly laugh. Then he stood up suddenly and put an arm around Timmy's shoulders.

"Do you know what I told him, Timmy boy?" he exclaimed. "I told him if he'd complained about any other man in the office, myself included, I'd have run a check. But not on Timmy Colt. No, sir." With his free hand he brushed the blueprint aside. "Hell, we all make mistakes. You'd have picked that one up ten times over before the final draft."

But Timmy only shook his head stubbornly.

"I think it's unwarranted to assume that, sir."

Mr. Hazard removed his protecting arm.

"What's wrong with you, anyway?" he asked with a touch of sharpness. "Have you lost your sense of humor?"

Timmy, to my horror, turned on him.

"How about Liendecker's sense of humor?" he asked, almost savagely. "He hasn't lost his by any chance, has he?"

Mr. Hazard raised his eyebrows and gave a low whistle.

"You'd better get back to your office, my boy," he said in a warning tone. "And do a little hard thinking about what happens to people who take themselves too seriously."

When I followed Timmy out the door I knew that the job had ceased to be a job. It had become an issue of infinitely larger dimensions.

"Liendecker's got me this time," he said grimly as we retraversed the long corridor. "But I'll see him in Hell before he catches me again!"

"He's worried about his six million," I quoted back to him. "You can't blame him, really. I think I'd feel the same way."

Timmy, however, was beyond the stage of being kidded.

"I'm going to get out all the papers in this God-damn deal," he continued, "and recheck every last one of them."

The waste of it, after all we'd done, appalled me.

"What does it matter what that guy thinks of you, Timmy?" I protested. "It's what Hazard thinks that counts. You know you're square with him."

He simply looked at me as if I couldn't know what I

was saying and turned off into the library. More than his humor had deserted him; his sense of proportion was gone. In the next few days he turned into a grim, driven creature who lived on sandwiches and coffee in a paper-cluttered office that he never seemed to leave. One night he didn't even go home, and when Flora came down in the morning to check up she found him asleep at his desk. After she had waked him and sent him to the washroom to shave, she came to my office.

"We've got to do something, Peter!" she exclaimed. "We've got to stop him. He's killing himself!"

"The job's almost over, Flora," I reminded her. "Take it easy."

"But this Liendecker's a fiend! Do you *know* that?"

I shrugged.

"I guess that's as good a term as any."

"And do you know *why* he's a fiend?" She leaned forward, both elbows now on my desk, her eyes glaring at me. "Because he sees Timmy the way Timmy sees himself! As sloppy and shiftless and no good!"

I stared.

"Is *that* the way Timmy sees himself?"

"Certainly it is!" she exclaimed. "The only way he gets through any job is with constant pats on the back. He's like a child, Peter. But just let one man like Liendecker get at him — well, it's the end. He'll take that man's opinion of him against all the world!"

I sat looking out the window after she had left and pondered her concept of Liendecker as a devil especially created to prod poor Timmy at his vulnerable point. I thought of him in Timmy's office, watching with the eye that seemed to anticipate error, dropping dry little reminders about the error in the deed and expressing and re-expressing his hope that all this "paper work" was not going to cost him his deal. It almost seemed to me that Flora might be right, that he and Timmy were like two cogged wheels, meshed to each other and moving ahead with a grim acceleration that must surely end in the destruction of one. But what could we do? It was a form of self-destruction that was eminently respectable.

Yet it ended, and nothing terrible seemed to have happened. We closed on schedule, and the closing itself was as simple as the preparations had been complicated. There were twenty of us sitting about the long table in the conference room of Everett & Coates, each with a large manila envelope which we opened on a given signal, transferring the previously executed documents to and fro between ourselves in accordance with a rehearsed pattern. It was like a Japanese comedy, a crazy pantomime as the finale of six weeks' madness. When it was over Mr. Liendecker himself walked slowly around the table and shook each of us, starting with Timmy, by the hand.

That night Liendecker gave a party for the people in his office and ours who had worked on the deal. I dined with Timmy and Flora at the Hazards', and we all went on to the Liendeckers' together. Their vast apartment, overlooking the East River, was a decorator's delight; its proprietors must have made a clean sweep of all former possessions before settling down to this harmony of gray and blue, of long low curving sofas and Mexican pottery and cream-colored tables with tiny legs. The guests, mostly from the company, moved timidly around in couples as they had come. Mrs. Liendecker, a small, nervous woman, hurried about ineffectually, asking people what they wanted to drink, while her husband stood aloof by the fireplace surrounded by a respectful half circle of younger men. It struck me that Mr. Hazard, with his broad teeth-baring grin, greeting the younger officers of American Export with a grip on the arm or shoulder, an approach of his large head and a snap of the eyelids, and his wife serenely following, almost a Roman matron in her plain gray evening dress, with her plain gray unwaved hair, seemed much more the host and hostess. They moved as easily through the constrained atmosphere of the room as though the Liendeckers had been their oldest friends and office parties their daily fare, yet I knew from dinner that Mrs. Hazard had only come when her husband had warned her, with just a hint of the peremptory behind his smile: "I think it might help, dear. These people are touchy." I wondered, if one's manners were good enough and one's belief in oneself sufficient, whether there might be no such thing in the world as compromise.

I walked with Timmy over to the bar table. He was extremely moody, and we had both been drinking steadily since our arrival at the Hazards' an hour before dinner.

"Well, it's over," I said.

"It's over," he agreed gloomily. "And you can say it now. Go ahead. I'm a martinet. I'm a fuss-budget."

"You're a martinet. You're a fuss-budget," I said obediently.

He gave me a bleak look.

"But we got it finished, didn't we? And finished right?"

"We got it finished," I repeated. "And finished right."

"Oh, go soak your head," he retorted.

I left him to his mood and crossed the room to where Flora was sitting alone on a beige sofa.

"Golly, what a ghastly party," she whispered. "Sit with me, Peter."

"You don't go out to sit with old friends," I reminded her.

"Don't you? *I* do."

"But you shouldn't. You should mingle."

"With this crowd?"

"It's good business," I said, sitting down. "Isn't this what business is?" I looked vaguely around at the looped yellow curtains, the long sofa opposite with its triangular pile of blue and white cushions. "Would you like to know what this room cost? I can tell you. I saw it in our files."

Flora looked severe. "Then you have no business telling people."

"But I *want* to tell you. I trust you." I looked at her as gravely as I could. "The responsibility of being the only one to know is too much for me."

Flora finally smiled, if a bit wearily.

"All right, Peter. How much?"

"Thirty-thousand," I whispered. "Not, of course, including the flower painting in the corner. That's by Mrs. Liendecker herself and is, naturally, priceless."

"What a snob you are, Peter."

"It is you, Flora, who disdain to mingle."

"But that's different," she insisted. "These people aren't *me*. I don't understand them."

"You mean you don't like them," I corrected her.

"Well, really, Peter," she said indignantly, "what have I in common with a man who spends more on one room than I could spend on my family in three years?"

"What in common? Your husband, of course."

She puckered her brow at this, and I couldn't help smiling. It seemed so buried in the past already, the whole terrible job, and I almost felt that Mr. Liendecker's whisky made up for it, tinging with a vaguely nostalgic quality the long rushed days behind.

"Well, we're through, anyway," she said with a sigh. "Drink to that with me, Peter. We're through with the whole damn thing." She clicked her glass against mine. "And he never blew up once, thank God."

Her tone made me look at her.

"What do you mean, Flora," I asked, "the *whole* damn thing?"

She hesitated.

"Why, the job, of course."

"Flora, I've seen you after too many of these jobs — " As I paused, staring at her, the light broke. "But of course! Timmy's been made a partner! That's it, isn't it!"

Flora turned very red and glanced quickly over in Mr. Hazard's direction.

"I never said that, Peter."

"You didn't have to! Can I congratulate him? I won't tell anyone."

"Peter!" She jumped up and put her hands on my

shoulders to force me back on the sofa. "Listen, you idiot, he doesn't *know* yet! Mr. Hazard whispered it to me when we were coming up in the elevator. He promised me once that when it happened I'd be the first to know."

I stared.

"And when does he tell Timmy? Or doesn't he?"

"Tonight. After the party. Now, Peter, be an angel and hang on to your tongue. In fact, don't have anything more to drink. You might leak it."

"Isn't that asking rather a lot? At a party?"

But I was not to know her answer for at that moment we heard the sharp insistent tinkle of spoons against glasses and Mr. Liendecker's voice authoritatively calling for silence.

"Has everyone got a glass?" he demanded in the tone of a scoutmaster asking his boys if each has his knapsack. He paused to let the waiters recirculate with fresh trays. "Everyone must have a glass because it's bad luck not to join in a toast, and I want to propose one. A toast to the boys who worked on the Jersey plant deal. They did a grand job, as I'm sure you all know — now just a second, just a second," he added testily as there were several "hear, hears" and glasses were prematurely raised. "First I want to tell you something about these fellas so you'll know what the hell you're drinking to." This reproach was followed by a mild, slightly nervous titter from the group. "It's only polite to start with the guys who aren't actually in the outfit, the lawyers and bakers and candlestick makers, and I guess the first one up to bat is Timmy Colt of Everett & Coates. I think most of you have met Timmy in the course of this deal, but I'm sure none of you have had a chance to observe him more closely than I have. We've been closeted together, Timmy and I, day after day and sometimes night after night, and I don't think I'm blowing my horn too loudly, Timmy, if I say that there were moments when even your young legal mind was glad to have the assistance of something a bit older and wiser. Isn't that so, Tim, my boy? We have to learn that theory isn't everything, don't we?"

Timmy was standing alone by the fireplace, one elbow resting on the edge of the mantel. He simply folded his arms across his chest and stared back at his host with expressionless eyes. I felt Flora's hand on my arm and the sudden intake of her breath.

"I hope we can take silence for assent," Mr. Liendecker continued briskly with an odd little gleam. "And I think I know our Timmy well enough to say that we can. I also thinks he knows how much we all appreciate the grand job that his firm has done and won't mind my telling you a little anecdote about how I caught him trying to save a bit of the new plant for the sellers." He paused with the tentative, anticipatory half smile of one about to tell a funny story. "It was the kind of thing that could have happened to anyone, you understand, particularly after the pace we'd all been going at, and I'm only giving old Timmy a poke in the ribs. Well, anyway, it seems that when the deed was being drawn — "

I sat in a trance of fascinated hate as Mr. Liendecker picked his leisurely, tedious way through the tired old story of the missing fraction of an acre. My animosity, thanks to the scotch, seemed to have detached itself from my heart;

it hung in the middle of the room, almost observable to myself, like a small black cloud over Mr. Liendecker's head, as real and corporate as his malice had become to me. When I glanced about the room I could see that my reaction was not unshared; I caught the communal sense, in nervous movements and exchanged glances, of the unfitness of such an anecdote at such a time. But Liendecker, of course, didn't mind that; he might even have enjoyed it. He stood there with his small smile that had become a mixture of complacency and sarcasm, like a lion tamer who cracks his whip with an easy, almost relaxed motion of the arm at the big demoralized cats that sit on stools around him, turning their heads away and opening their mouths in soundless snarls.

He had finished on a note that was again a jovial question to Timmy, some shabby disguise of good nature, and in the ensuing silence I heard Flora's agonized whisper in my ear.

"Dear God, this *is* the end. It really is."

And almost as she said it we heard Timmy's voice coming to us, cold and sarcastic, across the room, with only a slight tremble to show the passion behind his words.

"Mr. Liendecker has been good enough to recognize the individual nonentities behind the scenes. He shouldn't bother with them. What are they, after all, but hacks, as he has so easily demonstrated? If you must all drink toasts, drink them to Mr. Liendecker, his own financier, his own lawyer, his own priest, and if there's any justice in the after life — which I very much doubt — his own hell."

In the stupefied silence that followed this outburst Timmy marched across the room to the sofa where we were sitting.

"Come on, Flora," he said abruptly. "Let's get out of here."

She almost ran from the room ahead of him as conversation exploded nervously around their departing figures. Everybody suddenly spoke or filled a glass or lit a cigarette; they had rushed to their stations, like the disciplined crew of a suddenly foundering vessel, and could be counted on to wait, their life jackets neatly tied, for the order to abandon ship. Above the clamor I could hear Mr. Liendecker's laugh, high and harsh, and I caught a glimpse of him, his arm around another man's shoulders, his head tilted back, surrendering to the apparent uncontrollability of his mirth and protesting, between loud gasps, that some people, particularly lawyers, could just *never* take a joke.

I turned in misery to the bar table and was well on my way through a double scotch when I heard Mrs. Hazard's voice behind me.

"Dear me, you young people must have strong heads to take those things."

I spun around and stared sullenly at her high, clear forehead. Even her husband could not have scared me now.

"Maybe I need them."

"Maybe," she said, smiling. There was no reproach, even implied, in her eyes.

"You think I should stop?"

It was wonderful how little my rudeness seemed to surprise her.

"My arithmetic is simple. I think two scenes might be twice as bad as one."

"And you think I'm going to make another?"

"I think a good and loyal friend *might* make another,

yes," she said with a little nod. "And I think it might be wise if we took the good and loyal friend home before he did."

She simply looked out of the window as if she cared for nothing as much as the vessels on the East River, while I stubbornly finished my drink. Then she turned toward the door, and I found myself following her, with a dumb surprise that she should so assume my obedience. In the hall we found Mr. Hazard, who had actually managed to discover my hat and coat, and in three more minutes we were moving rapidly uptown in a taxi on the East River Drive.

I must have had even more to drink than I thought, for all the way home I appealed sentimentally to Mr. Hazard.

"You've no idea, sir, what that fiend put Timmy through," I kept protesting. "You *couldn't* because you weren't there. And Timmy was so patient! I've never seen anything to equal it. Because of you, Mr. Hazard! He did it for *you*. He looks upon you as a father!"

Mr. Hazard, sitting beside me, stared out of the window and said nothing. Yet there was just the suspicion of a smile on his lips, enough, anyway, to inspire me in my intoxication with the heart-filling hope that the world, the real world, might be what it then seemed, a place of unbreakable friendships before whose high gates the jackal Liendeckers skulked in vain.

"He wants an apology, of course," Mr. Hazard said suddenly. "He told me that when we left. He made it very clear that if he doesn't get it, either Timmy goes or he goes."

"Then let *him* go!" I cried passionately, going so far as

to grip his arm. "Oh, Mr. Hazard, if you only *knew* how Timmy needs backing up! His heart broke tonight. It was the last straw, before all those people! Of course, I know, sir, Mr. Liendecker's an important client, but you have lots of important clients, and Timmy will bring you plenty more. Truly, he will, sir!"

When Mr. Hazard finally turned to look at me, he was still smiling, but he was smiling, I made out with a sinking heart, only at the violence of my appeal. To him it was the scotch, of course, what but the scotch? And when I glanced suddenly at Mrs. Hazard and saw that she, too, had caught her husband's eye to exchange with him that same smile, I could only feel in a dull, defeated way that my world, scotch-inspired, was a thousand times braver and better than theirs.

"You forget something, Peter," Mr. Hazard said, putting a large hand on my shoulder and speaking in the paternal tone that I had heard him use to Timmy. "You forget that Tim treated us to a shocking breach of manners in the house of a man who was not only our client but our host. There's never any question about my backing Timmy up — I've always done that — but to back him up in the way that you suggest would be doing him a disfavor. Whatever I do, Peter, I shall be acting more for Timmy than for Sam Liendecker. You can bet on that."

We had pulled up before the old brownstone where my apartment was.

"And you won't mention this around the office tomorrow, will you, Peter?" he added.

"Oh, Mr. Hazard," I protested, getting out. "What do you take me for?"

The next morning, just before lunch, I walked down the corridor to Timmy's office. The door was closed, which was unusual in Everett & Coates, for much was made there of the advantages of an open and friendly atmosphere. When I went in I found Timmy sitting with his swivel chair turned toward the window, his feet resting on the radiator, his hands locked at the back of his head. He didn't even turn around as I entered.

"It's me," I said as the door closed behind. "What about lunch?"

He said nothing, and I sat down in the chair by his desk and played with the black pen in the inkstand. When he spoke he still didn't turn around.

"They want me to apologize to that son of a bitch."

"They?"

"Hazard, of course," he answered in the same clipped tone. "The great Hazard himself. The maker of graduation addresses. The high priest of the intellect. He wants me to grovel before that psychological louse."

There was a hardness in his tone that made me wonder if he or Hazard would suffer ultimately most by what might happen.

"And, of course, you won't."

He turned at this, his feet coming off the radiator with a bang, his eyes sharp.

"Would you?"

"No." I shrugged my shoulders. "But what does that amount to? I haven't your future. I haven't Flora and the boys. I don't even have Mr. Hazard. I can afford the luxury of not apologizing to men like Liendecker."

"You think it's only a luxury?"

"Fundamentally."

"You don't see the issue of personal integrity?"

"I see it. I don't see it as inevitable."

He turned away again to the window.

"I would never have thought you so slippery, Peter."

But there was no point going into this.

"How did Hazard put it to you?" I asked. "Was it 'or else'?"

"No. He simply asked me to. But it's obvious how I'll stand here if I don't."

I nodded slowly and then sighed.

"You see too much black and white, Timmy," I said. "You forget that life can be gray, too. Even a Liendecker can be gray."

"If you're Liendecker's lawyer," he snapped, "you can sing his praises in someone else's office."

I nodded again, but only to the back of his head, and left. During the next few days none of us saw him at all. He arrived in the office in the middle of the morning and left usually in the middle of the afternoon. With his door always shut, people were quick to catch the idea that his mood, to put it mildly, was unsociable. Besides, the news of his outburst at the Liendeckers' had by now leaked from American Export and was all over the office. Associates were continually coming into my office to hear the story at first hand. I tried to minimize it, but it was the kind of story that defied minimization. They would leave with a delighted expression of "Hot damn!" and for all Timmy's popularity and the universal sympathy with his predicament, I found I was envied as the one who has seen the trapeze artist fall, the matador gored.

Mr. Hazard never referred to the scene in the taxicab, but he treated me very cordially now and even called me into his office one day to describe a simple codicil that his wife needed to cover a piece of jewelry that she had just inherited from an aunt. Ordinarily he would have channeled any such business through my department head, and I was flattered and pleased at such a mark of confidence. He quite took his time about the small problem involved and asked me questions with a charming deference to what he purported to consider my superior technical knowledge on the subject. It was a most satisfactory interview, and when I rose to leave he asked me about Timmy.

"How do you find him?"

"He won't talk to me," I said. "I can't help."

"I can't help either," he said with a sigh. "No one can really help Timmy but himself. He's like a stubborn child. One leaves him alone on the theory that he'll eventually come out of it. I suppose there's always the danger that he won't. But I can't understand the pleasure he gets in pounding his head against a stone wall and then rubbing it to look for blood. Can you, Peter?"

I knew that it was the wrong answer, but I couldn't help it.

"Yes, sir. I can understand it."

"Can you really?" He smiled, a touch more coolly, and then nodded to conclude our interview. "Maybe you can persuade him, then, that it's an unprofitable experience."

When I went uptown the following afternoon to Mrs. Hazard's to go over with her a draft of the codicil, I was told by the maid that she was still out, and I waited for her in her husband's dark, leathery library, walking slowly about with the awe that the room's silent, clock-ticking atmosphere induced and peering at the overframed forest scenes individually lighted with a care that seemed hardly merited. When I heard the unexpected sound of small children in the hall and went to the door, I was startled to see Timmy's two boys disappearing into the dining room. I was still staring after them when I heard a woman's heels on the stairway and, looking up, saw Flora. She was wearing a hat and coat and uttered a little cry when she saw me.

"Peter! What are *you* doing here?"

"It seems to me that I'm the one who ought to ask that question."

She hurried down the remaining steps and pushed me into the library ahead of her.

"I've had enough," she said abruptly. "I've had all I can take. I'm going away."

"And leaving the boys *here?*"

"Mrs. Hazard said I could," she said defiantly. "She's always been like a mother to me. The way he's been a father to Timmy. Who else could I go to?"

I caught her by the hand.

"Wait a second, please, Flora! You mean you're leaving Timmy. *Now!*"

She pulled her hand away.

"That's his decision!" she exclaimed. "Not mine. Mrs. Hazard will know where to find me. He can come and get me whenever he wants. Whenever he's made up his mind to stop behaving like a spoilt child."

I stared.

"You mean about Liendecker? You'll make him apologize? But this is blackmail, Flora!"

"Then I've come to blackmail," she retorted grimly. "There we are." Her expression changed, however, when she took in mine. "What else can I do, Peter?" she pleaded. "How else can I save him? He won't even talk to me about it any more, because he thinks I'm not on his side." There were sudden tears in her eyes. "He's determined to rook his life over this foolish issue. He gets some kind of savage pleasure out of counting up the people who have deserted him, as he puts it, starting with Mr. Hazard and — "

"But there are other firms, Flora," I protested. "Timmy can always get a job. Don't make him pay a price he doesn't want to pay!"

She shook her head again, her eyes closed for the moment, as if she had been through the whole thing too many times to reopen the door.

"There aren't other firms for Timmy," she said firmly. "Not in his present mood. That firm is his life. And I'm not going to stand by and see him throw it away, just to spite Mr. Liendecker."

"But is this going to stop him?"

"As I say, that's for him to decide," she said, turning away. "It will either bring him to his senses or — or give him another jewel for that martyr's crown of his."

"But if it doesn't," I protested desperately, following her as she went down to the front door, "if he bangs out of the firm and starts drinking himself to death — "

"Then I'll come back to him, of course," she said, turning back to me and holding her hand out. "Only don't tell *him* that, Peter Westcott."

When Mrs. Hazard came in, a few minutes later, she found me still in the hall and stunned.

"Flora told me," I said at once, hurrying over to her. "I met her here. Tell me, Mrs. Hazard, do you think it's a good idea?"

Mrs. Hazard paused while she took off her hat, pulling out the long pin with the mother-of-pearl end and placing it on the table.

"Do I? Not in the least."

"Can't you do something about it?" I paused, suddenly embarrassed at my own impertinence. "Can't you make Mr. Hazard do something, I mean?"

"Well, if I leave *him*, Peter," she said, smiling at me, "where can I send my own children?"

Timmy came into my office the following morning and banged the door shut behind him. He looked as if he had not slept, and his eyes jumped at me angrily.

"I'm going over to apologize to Liendecker," he said. "I want you to come along as a witness to tell the world that I did it properly. No matter what *he* says afterwards."

All the way down in the elevator and during the two-block walk to American Export we hardly exchanged a word. Timmy walked a little bit ahead of me, pausing from time to time impatiently for me to catch up.

"Let's not be all day," he muttered once. "Let's get this damn thing over with, shall we?"

At American Export, Mr. Liendecker's secretary told us, with a tailored friendliness, that the president would see us in a few minutes. We were then kept waiting, despite

Timmy's appointment, a full half-hour. I would have been almost disappointed in Mr. Liendecker had he not insisted on this final touch. His greatest strength lay in the fact that he never, no matter how regularly or at what interest a debt was paid, forgave the least portion of the unpaid balance. One knew, at least, where one stood with him. Finally I turned to Timmy.

"Is Flora back?"

He didn't look at me.

"She's back," he said briefly. "And I'm here."

"I know what this must be costing you, Timmy."

This time he looked at me, but his look was withering. A light on the secretary's desk flashed green, and she cried, as if she, too, could be happy at our good news, "Mr. Liendecker will see you now, gentlemen!"

He was leaning back in his big brown leather chair, his hands folded behind his head. When we had been seated in front of him he leaned suddenly forward and put his elbows on the desk. His eyes ran restlessly over the blotter, and he closed and opened the top of the silver inkwell. I could see the note on which he was going to play the scene, the note of faint boredom, of "what's this all about," the implication that it was we and not he who were making mountains out of molehills. And, to do even him justice, it may have been sincere. He had won, that was obvious, and it was one of the tragedies of men of his type that if defeat was unendurably galling, victory was not proportionately sweet.

"Well, gentlemen?"

Timmy went straight to the point.

"I've come to apologize, sir, for my rudeness of the other night." He gave the rug at this point a long, hard look. "Obviously, I wouldn't have come for any other reason. I won't say that I don't know what got into me. I do. I blew up at a perfectly harmless joke. I can only blame it on the nervous fatigue that followed the sale."

Mr. Liendecker glanced up at this.

"We *all* worked pretty hard on that sale, Colt."

"I know it," Timmy agreed, nodding. "You harder than anyone, Mr. Liendecker. And, after all, you had the responsibility of the whole thing. I have a lot to learn from you, sir, both in manners and in patience."

I drew in my breath and glanced out of the corner of my eye at Timmy. But he looked perfectly serious. Mr. Liendecker, who had evidently shared my suspicion, looked at him shrewdly for a moment and then grunted.

"It pays to know how to hang on to your temper, young fella," he said. "You've found that out. Okay. I wouldn't be surprised if you were the kind who only had to find it out once."

"Thank you, sir. I'll remember that."

"I guess he will, at that," Mr. Liendecker said more cheerfully now, rising and turning to me. "What about it, Westcott?"

"I'm sure he will, sir," I answered, getting up. "I'm sure that anyone who can make such a handsome apology will not forget the small slip that occasioned it."

Mr. Liendecker's gray eyes ran over me for just a moment, and then he turned back to Timmy.

"I'll call Hazard this morning, son," he said, shaking his

hand, "and tell him I want our next job at Everett &
Coates handled by you. Okay? Good day, gentlemen."

Outside in the lobby as we waited for the elevator
Timmy looked at me sullenly.

"You almost fixed my wagon that time," he muttered.
"Who asked you to stick up for me, anyway?"

"I thought if you groveled any more you'd be under the
rug," I retorted. "Did you have to go *that* far?"

"That's nothing to how far I'm going," he said roughly.
"Not by a long shot, brother."

The printed card announcing that Mr. Timothy Colt had
been made a member of the firm was sent out through the
downtown legal world no less than two weeks after our
fateful interview with Mr. Liendecker. I have known
lawyers to whom the advent of partnership has been a
source of almost hourly satisfaction for as much as a year
afterwards, men in whose faces one could see the reflection
of that bright little thought, ceaselessly reiterated like the
chirp of a starling: "I'm a partner! I'm a partner!" Timmy,
however, seemed to take the news very coolly. He barely
smiled at us when we went to congratulate him and appeared already to have given his entire attention to the
business of moving into his new office and getting started
on his next job. The past was evidently not a field in which
he intended to allow himself even a civilized loiter.

Such brisk efficiency, even for him, came as a surprise to
the office, but what really astonished the associates was the
change in his attitude toward us. He had always deplored
the barrier between the partner and clerk and insisted that

if he was ever promoted, he would not do as so many did, cultivate old friendships for the first year and then gradually, through inertia, pressure of work and the opening up of new peaks, relax his democratic impulses and accept the "Mr." accorded him by the younger clerks as his natural due. But now, on the contrary, he seemed willing to skip even this year of labored intimacy and to retire to an aloofness behind closed doors that made Mr. Hazard himself appear the artist of the common touch. When younger men were called to his office it was by his secretary, never himself, and it was to find a detached, distant Mr. Colt leaning over a paper on his desk, one hand propping his brow, who simply raised his eyes to acknowledge their entrance and, cutting through the usual salutations, started at once on business. In all too brief a time, the time it takes in any organization to substitute a bad reputation for a good one, Timmy became the partner for whom we all least cared to work. It was not that he was actually disagreeable or even that he lost his temper, but he would pass his hand over his eyes when asked to explain something and pause for a moment of silence that filled the room with the atmosphere of his repressed exasperation. Then he would answer in slow, meticulous syllables that only hammered into his poor listener's head the low opinion that he had formed of his intellect. "I trust it is clear," he would say, looking up at last, "*now?*"

My first contact with this treatment came by an unhappy chance when Timmy, checking the library files on an obscure point of tax law, chanced upon an old memorandum that I had written just after I had come into the office.

It was my first postwar job, and it contained a mistake which no one had picked up at the time. Timmy, of course, fell right into it.

"But I don't understand," he kept repeating to me. "Your conclusion is in direct contravention to the leading case on the subject. Direct. I don't understand."

"It's not so hard to understand," I replied. "The memorandum is simply wrong, that's all. Is that so fantastic?"

Timmy became even more the partner at this.

"In our files, Peter Westcott," he said, looking up at me sternly, "I very much hope that it *is* fantastic."

I said nothing.

"You don't even seem surprised," he pursued, "when I point out the contradiction. Are you in the habit of seeing your memoranda so easily rebutted?"

"I knew about the contradiction," I said sullenly. "It occurred to me after the memo was filed."

"Indeed? And may I ask, then, why you failed to correct it?"

"I never thought anyone would read it," I said with a sigh. "And I didn't want to stir the matter up. You know how it is, Timmy. You haven't been a partner *that* long."

He gave me a straight look.

"If you're implying that it was my habit as an associate to leave memoranda in the files which I knew to be misleading —"

"Do you know what's happening to you, Timmy?" I interrupted angrily. "You're becoming a Scrooge! Everyone says so. But if you think I'm a Bob Cratchit, it's going to take more than a Christmas turkey to win me around!"

Timmy continued to gaze at me for a moment with faintly curious eyes and then glanced down again at the offending memorandum.

"Oh, go soak your head," he said.

It was not long after this, although in no way because of it, that I resigned from Everett & Coates to take a legal job in a publishing company that was one of their clients and where I could at least count on evenings and weekends for my own writing. Ordinarily Timmy would have been the first person whom I would have consulted before making such a decision, but as things were, I allowed him to hear of it after it had become an accomplished fact. I'm afraid, indeed, that I got a perverse satisfaction out of imagining that his feelings might be hurt. He came himself to my office, which he hadn't done since his promotion, and, leaning back in a chair, put his feet up on my desk.

"This is sudden news that I heard at the partners' lunch today, Peter," he said with a little smile. "I rather thought that you and I might have discussed it."

"I saw no reason, Timmy. My mind was made up. And, besides, you're always so busy."

His little smile didn't change. It seemed to be offered up to me as a concession to his own shyness, even as a barrier against anything that I might throw.

"You don't exactly have a dim future here, you know."

"In spite of inaccurate memoranda?"

He shrugged his shoulders.

"In spite of them."

Well, it was the olive branch, of course, or as close to

it as Timmy could fashion one, and maybe it was churlish of me not to have accepted it, but I was too angry at his recent neglect and too disgusted at what he seemed to have done to himself to let him off so easily. We continued to chat but in a desultory manner, and I felt that he was quietly taking in both me and my attitude as further examples of the unreasonable but utterly predictable injustice of this world.

He must have told Flora that night of my decision, for the next afternoon I had a wonderful letter from her, full of warmth and congratulation, applauding my resolution to give up the downtown world and even looking forward to the day when I should abandon my new employer and make writing my full-time occupation.

"I hope that we'll see you," she ended, "and that it won't be as it is with others who have left the firm, simply an exchange of Christmas cards. But then I've learned not to be unreasonable about what life does. Do try, however, to come and see me. As you can tell by the letterhead, we've moved to a swankier apartment. At least Timmy thinks it's swankier. He seems to be suffering these days from an acute case of mammon. Anything you want to know about us in the future you can find in the social columns. P.S. I *loathe* it. P.P.S. So does he, only he won't admit it!"

It was several months before I found out what Flora meant by Timmy's "acute case of mammon." My new job, as it turned out, was by no means exclusively legal; I was the general assistant and handy man of the chairman of the board and as such had to go with him to various social affairs, usually cocktail parties for worthy causes and less worthy people given in the private suites of large hotels. On one such occasion I encountered Timmy. He was entirely agreeable and made no allusion to any former unpleasantness between us; he inquired politely about my new business, but instead of listening to my answers, his eyes roamed the room alertly. From time to time he interrupted me, without the least apology, to ask if I knew this or that person whom he would point out.

"Now who is that lady?" he asked, gesturing toward a tall thin woman in black.

"That's Lorna Treadway."

"And why is she here?"

"Lorna? She goes everywhere."

Timmy frowned, the way he did at the office when somebody failed to understand the purport of his question.

"Yes, but why? I understand she writes a column on decorating. Is it for that?"

"Lord, no. That column's a joke. Lorna's just one of those people whom other people always have around. You know how it is."

He shook his head.

"Someone told me she had quite a social position."

I stared at him.

"Timmy, what's come over you? You can't start talking like that. Even if you *are* a partner."

"Clients don't grow on trees, you know."

"But you're not a client getter," I protested. "You're not even the type!"

"We'll see about that," he said coolly. "Everyone thinks

I'd be perfectly satisfied to be known all my life as Hazard's helper. Well, they're wrong. You don't get to know the people who count by holing yourself up in a two-by-four office all day."

"Oh. Sam Liendecker. I see all."

"Well, Sam makes a lot of sense on these things," he retorted, obviously nettled. "I went up to Canada on a fishing trip with him last spring, and we met Harris Grant. You know, the oil man. Well, Grant didn't even know that right in Everett & Coates we happen to have one of the best legal oil specialists in the country — "

I could see, as he talked, that he had brought to his new social activities the same careful literal-mindedness that I had seen him bring to his contracts and mergers. It was a job like other jobs, wasn't it? And being done, directly or indirectly, for the firm? Which to his way of thinking, I supposed, more than took care of other issues involved.

"What does Mr. Hazard think of your new activities?" I couldn't help asking.

"Well, Hazard, of course, is an older man," he said with a slight frown. "He comes of a more secure world. And then, don't forget, he's Henry Hazard. Not an unknown like T. Colt." He turned and put his hand on my shoulder. "But to hell with this, Peter. How about coming home for a drink? Flora hasn't seen you in ages."

I went uptown with him to the east sixties where they now lived. The apartment was a good size and of good proportions, but nothing could save it from the peculiar combination of emptiness and disorder that only the Colts knew how to bestow. There were a few handsome pieces, department store Chippendale, but theirs was a lonely show in the absence of a rug and before the bareness of walls broken only by a photograph of Timmy's wartime aircraft carrier. The children's cowboy paraphernalia lay scattered about, and beside the fireplace gleamed the wide gray vacancy of a television set.

"Flora!" Timmy called. "I've got a friend for you!"

I heard the sound of bedroom slippers in the corridor, and Flora came in, dressed in a flower-patterned wrapper, pushing her hair back. Her mouth fell open.

"Peter!" she cried and hurried over to kiss me, putting both arms around my neck. "Well, I'll be a son of a gun!"

Any other woman might have apologized for the state of the room, for her own state; not Flora. Her not doing so made it almost, if not completely, all right. Timmy went to mix drinks, and by the time he had come back I had told her more about myself and my job than I had told anyone since I had left Everett & Coates. When he handed her her whisky, however, he changed the subject.

"I looked in on the boys," he said. "Their colds seem better."

"Oh, they're much better."

"Then there's no reason you can't come with me to-night," he continued. "We might as well get some good out of that nurse."

Flora looked up in alarm.

"Oh, Timmy, I couldn't leave them! Not tonight!"

He stirred his drink slowly.

"Martha tells me their temperatures have been normal since yesterday," he observed.

"Yes, but, Timmy, you *know* how quickly they can jump!"

"Then she can call us. We'll be exactly five blocks away."

"Oh, Timmy, please! No!"

There was a pause while he looked at her steadily.

"Will you admit it's not the boys, then?" he asked quietly, glancing down again at his drink. "Will you have the fairness to admit it's because you don't want to go?"

"You *know* I don't want to go!"

"And that's your only reason?"

She took a long swallow of her drink and then looked back at him in sudden defiance.

"All right, it's my only reason. Name me a better." She turned around to me for support. "He wants me to go to the Liendeckers', Peter. You know I can't face that."

I gaped.

"Of course, you can't! What are you thinking of, Timmy?"

He leaned back on the sofa and crossed his arms on his chest. He was angry now, but I could see that it was one of those rich, prepared, satisfying angers.

"What was *she* thinking of, Peter," he asked me sharply, "when she made me go on my knees to Sam Liendecker?"

"Knees?" I retorted. "Really, Timmy, you're being absurd!"

Flora had turned pale.

"So that's it," she said. "You want to get back at me for that. You've always wanted to, haven't you? Ever since?"

"It isn't a question of getting back," he said, with a rather condescending patience. "It's simply a question of the decision you made at that time. The decision of the sort of life we were going to lead."

"*I* made that decision?" she demanded.

"Most effectively," he replied. "We *had* been the kind of people who wouldn't apologize to Sam Liendecker. Now we're not. You must face that, Flora. I can't let you go on with this illusion that because you stay at home with the children you've preserved your integrity. You're in this with me. Up to the hilt."

There was a heavy silence. Flora stared into the fireplace, holding her drink close to her lips and taking, from moment to moment, quick, abstracted sips.

"I want to be in anything you're in, Timmy," she said sadly. "I'm not trying to preserve any integrity that you don't think you have. I'll admit my responsibility for the apology to Liendecker, and I'll take the consequences. But why is this party a consequence? Unless *you* make it so?"

"Because it's the life you chose," he insisted. "If I've made a pact with the devil, please don't think that he's going to get his share of me for a junior partnership. Oh, no. I want my money's worth."

Flora looked at me pleadingly.

"Does it make any sense to you, Peter?"

"None whatever."

"You want me to bring home the money," Timmy continued, angered by our exchange, "but you don't want to know where it's from. Well, I won't let you get away with that. You're going to see for yourself!"

Flora shrugged her shoulders, as one who has suddenly given up.

"All right, I'll go to the damn party," she said wearily. "But on one condition. If Peter will go, too."

"*Me?* Why drag me into it? I'm not even asked!"

"It's all right," she assured me. "We'll take you. Timmy's friend, Sam, will be delighted. Won't he, Timmy?"

He looked at her in surprise.

"As a matter of fact, he will," he agreed. "I think he liked you, Peter."

"I'm sorry I can't return the compliment."

"Oh, please, Peter." Flora got up and came over to sit on the arm of my chair. "Come for my sake. I want to have *one* friend there."

She glanced at Timmy as she said this.

"Thank you," he said grimly.

I allowed myself to be persuaded, mostly to avoid what I thought might at any moment turn into a serious row. I went home to dress and make myself a sandwich; like the other Liendecker affair, it was a late evening party. When I got back to the Colts' a little before ten Flora opened the door. She was wearing a plain evening dress, of her customary brown, and was holding an old-fashioned glass in one hand.

"I'm getting in a gala mood," she said, raising the glass. "Are you in a gala mood, Peter?"

"Well, don't overdo it," I warned her. "Remember what happened *last* time we were at the Liendeckers'."

"Don't you think it's my turn?" she demanded. "Don't you think *I* should insult him this time?"

"Maybe we'd better *not* go to this party."

She laughed, rather too loudly.

"You're afraid I will, aren't you, Peter? But why not? As long as I apologize, the way he did. Then we'll be in the same boat, won't we?" She shrugged her shoulders and turned back into the living room. "Who knows? We might even be able to forgive each other."

Timmy appeared at the door to the bedroom corridor, buttoning the coat of his double-breasted midnight-blue tuxedo.

"Hi, Peter," he said casually, "are we about ready?" Then he saw the drink in Flora's hand and his expression changed. He crossed the room and took it from her. "What are you trying to do, anyway? Get potted?"

"It might help," she retorted and turned back into the hall to get her coat.

The Liendeckers' party was large, and I didn't know a soul there. Mr. Liendecker's social ambitions were not as specific as his business ones; he was not, as far as I could see, striking for any particular group or stratum. I suspect that to him "society" was a thing you had sent in when you gave a party, provided, so to speak, by a caterer with the little red-coated orchestra and the champagne. Where he actually got his guests I don't know; the women were pretty enough, but they had a hard, manicured look and the men with them in most cases seemed to be older. I am not, however, making insinuations; they were probably mostly married just as they were probably mostly childless, the inhabitants of apartment hotels and night clubs, with big incomes consumed in evanescent luxury, the type of new-rich who abound in New York, curiously satisfied with the little that their money buys.

Mr. Liendecker greeted me enthusiastically; it was one

of his characteristics that he never forgot a name. He then put a firm hand on Timmy's elbow and led him off to introduce him to Lorna Treadway. Flora and I, abandoned, sat side by side in a corner, and I noticed disapprovingly how quickly she reached for the darkest whisky on a passing tray. She looked sullen and even dowdy with her inadequately combed hair and those eyes, resentful and worried, darting from one to another of the well-dressed women who crossed and recrossed the floor in front of us. She drank off the whole glass while we made unkind comments about them. When she reached for another, however, I caught her hand.

"No, Flora. Really."

The waiter hesitated, embarrassed, and then moved off. When she looked at me, I saw the tears in her eyes.

"Oh, Peter, what good am I to him now?" she asked, slumping back on the sofa. "Shouldn't I pack up and get out and let him marry one of these sleeky creatures? No, I'm not fair," she continued, shaking her head with sudden firmness, "they're not really sleeky. It's just that I'm a mess. They're beautiful, really. And so is he. Isn't he, Peter?"

"Now, Flora."

"Oh, don't comfort me for God's sake, I can't stand it." She put her hands to her eyes for a moment. "Maybe he's right. Maybe I should never have forced him. Maybe I *have* been selfish in not taking part in this new life of his. But I can't, Peter, I simply can't. Not even for love, and God knows I love him. But some things are stronger than love. Oh, Peter, how many things are stronger than love! And when you realize that and still love, you want to die, that's all."

"You can't be someone you aren't, Flora," I said.

"Oh, I could do better." Dry-eyed again, she nodded her head briskly. "I could do a lot better. I could be more careful about my clothes, and I could make small talk. And I could flatter Mr. Liendecker. But I won't. I don't know why, but I won't. Timmy's right about me, Peter. I *am* selfish. Selfish and pigheaded. I made him do what I wouldn't do myself, God help me, and now I've been paid off in kind."

She swallowed suddenly, with difficulty.

"Are you all right, Flora?"

She stood up.

"I'm going to the ladies' room."

She was gone for some time, and I was beginning to feel concerned when I saw a maid hurry out of the door into which she had disappeared and cross the living room to whisper to Mrs. Liendecker. The latter looked startled; she drew herself up for a moment and glanced nervously about the room. Then she went over to Timmy and whispered for a moment in his ear. His expression did not change as he listened to her; he simply nodded and then turned with a firm step toward the door. I got up and hurried over to him.

"Timmy!"

He turned around.

"Yes?"

"Is Flora all right?"

"She's been sick," he said calmly and then paused for a second, adding, almost as an afterthought, "all over Mrs. Liendecker's bed."

For one wild moment I thought I was going to shriek with laughter.

"But she's okay?"

"She's okay *now*," he corrected me. "She was never a great one at holding her whisky. You remember that, Peter."

"Poor Flora."

"Poor me," he retorted. Then he glanced over my shoulder, almost curiously, at the crowded room behind me. "I think it could hardly be denied," he added in a more reflective tone, "that Flora and I are something less than assets at the Liendeckers' parties."

I had a sudden vision of her facing him later, pale and defeated, over the ruins of their evening.

"Oh, Timmy, you won't be hard on her, will you?" I begged. "You won't bawl her out?"

He gave me an odd, direct look that I couldn't interpret.

"What do you take me for?"

"Well, I simply — well — " I stopped in confusion.

"It's up to her," he explained, his eyes still fixed on me. "Don't you know that, Peter?"

I stared.

"Know what?"

"What Flora is to me," he said. "I want what she wants, Peter. Every time. But she has to make her mind up, you know. She has to make the decisions." He smiled suddenly, with the charm of the Timmy I had first known, the Timmy of romantic antecedents. "I rather imagine she's made another one just now."

But I knew, as he turned and I watched his straight

back retreat down the corridor toward Mrs. Liendecker's room, that the world would not let them go back now to the old life where they had been so happy, where he with each job and she with each uneventful day had lived as if the future with its bag of small duties and lip services had not loomed before them. No, that was the past, the past of their obscurity, when they had been idealists in a vacuum. Above them, around them, in the great world, adjustments had been made, concessions granted. But none of this had even existed for Timmy and Flora; the rudeness of their awakening had shown me that. There would be nothing easy for them, as for Mr. Hazard, in compromise, nothing of grace. It was a reproach to the very world which they would live in that poor Flora's single gesture of protest should have seemed so ludicrous.

THE EVOLUTION
OF
LORNA TREADWAY

.

The Evolution of Lorna Treadway

LORNA TREADWAY PASSED AS A GOOD-LOOKING WOMAN, and I suppose she was. Certainly she did everything for her looks that a woman could do. She dressed well and appropriately for her long, lanky body; and her mannerisms, her way of constantly running a fine white bony hand through her bobbed black hair and her habit of sticking her chin forward as she emphatically talked, made her seem as she wished to seem, intense but intelligent, sharp but sympathetic, disciplined but at the same time humorous, even democratic. Yet there was something about Lorna that made her closer friends, when I first knew her, speak of her as "poor Lorna." At first I took it that they referred to the fact that she had been abandoned for a much younger woman by the handsome sports-loving Bill Treadway, with whom, according to all reports, she was still very much in love, and this undoubtedly had been the origin of the epithet, but as I came to know her better, I realized that Lorna had earned it more by being the kind of woman whom a man like Bill would desert than by having been so deserted. For Lorna, despite a lonely need of men that was manifested in her almost absurd attentiveness, her many serious head-noddings, her ceaseless repetition of the phrase, "But you're so *right*" whenever she was talking to a male of any virility, was not attractive to them. She had too much the kind of charm that is admired by women, a sophisticated, fashion-magazine charm, long-limbed, pale-skinned, flat-breasted, wide-eyed. She cared too much and she tried too hard, with men and in everything else. The little suppers in her white and gold dining room were too self-consciously intimate; her column on "decorous living" in the Sunday paper too aggressively gay. She had suffered all the trials of the gallant little widow (except that she wasn't a widow): the amiable, improvident father who had died when she was young, the selfish mother who had spent the remainder of his money, the unfaithful and alcoholic husband. With a sketchy alimony and her newspaper column she now just managed to support herself and a small daughter who had asthma. But if she had been through too much, she had taken it too well; her courage had begun to bore. Friends made a point of seeing that her evenings were not lonely, of introducing her to prospective beaux, but despite this and despite the chatter all over her world to every unattached male of "I know just the girl for you, an angel," the masculine sex, with a baffling silent, inarticulate semi-loyalty to themselves and to the type of man that Bill Treadway was, refused to become involved with Lorna.

It was with great joy, therefore, that the rumor was spread around that poor Lorna had at last found a "real" beau. I was dining with her one night and had been about to ask about him when she forestalled me, in her bright, eager way.

"Have you met Harris?" she asked me. "Harris Grant?"

"No, but that's he, isn't it?" I nodded across the room in the direction of a short, rather stocky individual who appeared to be about fifty years of age. His large firm nose, his staring brown eyes and the thick shock of his gray hair seemed to shout in one's face that he was an executive. "I can see he's done well."

"He's made a small fortune in oil," she told me gravely. "And all since the war."

"By a small, I assume you mean a large."

"Oh, he's a sort of rough diamond, I admit," she went on, as if my remark had implied this. "But *real,* if you know what I mean. You'd like him, Peter. You like real people."

"I never could see how one human being could be any more real than another."

"Because he *does* things," she explained eagerly. "He's not like the rest of our friends, who deal with words all the time, just words, lawyers and advertisers and so on — not that there's anything wrong with words, dear Peter, certainly the way you use them — but you know Harris *makes* things, he's a builder in our society. And that's so much more important, isn't it, than whether or not he calls an evening dress a 'formal' or says 'drapes' instead of 'curtains'?"

"He doesn't make things," I pointed out. "He pumps them out of the ground."

"But you see what I mean," she insisted

I wasn't, however, going to let her get away with this. After all, it was her own column that had solemnly warned me against "drapes."

"Does he describe you as a 'gracious hostess'?" I asked,

remembering another of her famous "don'ts."

"Well, what if he does? Just what of it?"

"Don't get angry, Lorna. I'm one of your readers, that's all."

"*Those* things," she said with a contemptuous sweep of her hand, the gesture of one who has found a new enlightenment. "Why, Harris could learn those things in an afternoon."

"With you as a teacher."

"But you don't understand!" she exclaimed. "I don't want to teach him anything. I want him to teach *me!*"

After dinner she took me up and introduced me to her new friend. He made her repeat my name carefully, leaning his head closer as she did so and giving it a decided shake when he understood.

"Westcott," he repeated, as though now he would never forget it. "Westcott. Fine. I'm pleased to meet you, Westcott."

"Peter's a writer," Lorna coached him. "But don't let that put you off. He's not one of these artists who hates businessmen."

"A writer, eh," he said as Lorna moved off. "Fine. Grand. What sort of things do you write?"

"Oh, novels, stories," I said vaguely.

"About real people?"

"I hope not."

"I mean about real types," he corrected himself. "Do you write about society people, for example?"

"What sort of people?" I asked. This may have seemed fatuous of me, but his term was one so strongly outlawed by Lorna's column that it took me aback to hear it under her own roof.

"Why, you know," he said in surprise. "The people in this room. Aren't they society people?"

"Well, I suppose they are," I conceded. I wondered indeed, as I looked around, what other term would be more apt.

"You take them for granted, I see," he continued. "You weren't brought up in a mining town. Someday I'll tell you my story, Westcott. It would make a book. A tremendous book. Have you ever written a best-seller?"

I admitted that I had not.

"Well, there you are," he said. "It's probably your material."

"Do you like society people?" I ventured.

"I like Lorna," he came back at me promptly. "But she's the real thing. She's got something that can't be taught, you know what I mean? That touch you have to be born with. No, I'm not down on old families. People say they're snooty, I know. But maybe they've got something to be snooty about. That's what I want to find out."

If he really believed that Lorna's touch was unteachable, he may have had hopes of acquiring it by osmosis, for he soon became a fixture in her life. He escorted her wherever she went and appeared at all her suppers, and it became accepted practice to ask him to any party that Lorna was asked to. Her friends liked him at first. They took his naïveté for sincerity, his bluntness for honesty, his broad humor as the fresh, strong breeze of the western prairies. For they were people who prided themselves on not being "stuffy." Republicans, they supported Mr. Truman's foreign policy and deplored Senator McCarthy. Grotonians or St. Markers, they sent their sons to Exeter. They wanted for their children what they had had themselves, but they wanted it wrapped up in a package that bore the approving stamp of the progressive: the summer camp with the single Negro child, the small and out-of-the-way country place with the club that could take in everyone because everyone was only one group. They spoke of their parents and grandparents, who had been far richer than themselves, with affectionate amusement, laughing at the little snobbishnesses of the past as though such things were as quaint and dead today as Brewster town cars and spun sugar for ice cream, but their laughs, it always struck me, had a note of the reverential, their stories a vibrant chord of nostalgia. For this past seemed to overwhelm and make fun of them with its very magnitude; the Canaletto in the tiny hall had obviously been used to larger quarters, the diamond clip, so cleverly redesigned, had once been part of a tiara. Lorna's friends had to keep convincing themselves daily that theirs was a better show.

"You know what I can't understand about that crowd is the difference between the men and the women," Harris told me one night when he and Lorna and I were going home from a party in a taxi. "The women are fine. They'd fit in anywhere. But the men have lost their aggressiveness. They don't really want to compete any more. They're only interested in hanging on to what they've got."

Harris always assumed that as a writer I only frequented

this group to study it, a sort of Margaret Mead on a South Sea island.

"I think there's a great deal in what Harris says," Lorna said, nodding her head seriously, as she always did with men. "I think it's very sharp of him to see it. Don't you, Peter?"

"Women, I suppose, are more adaptable," I conceded. "That's why barbarians took off the women and children but killed the men, isn't it? There wasn't anything they could do with the men."

Harris put a stout arm playfully around Lorna's shoulders.

"Shall I sack your village and carry you off?" he demanded. "Would you like that, eh?"

Lorna giggled, obviously loving it.

"Well, you won't have to kill me first," I retorted, disgusted with both of them.

"Why, Peter!" Lorna protested, giggling again. "How rude of you!"

It was Harris's attitude toward the friends, not theirs toward him, that brought about the gradual diminution of his popularity. They never intended that their friendship, which they regarded as selectively, if democratically, given, should be casually accepted as a tribute to his financial success. Yet such was Harris's attitude. He appeared to believe that his money created actual social rights, that these people *had* to take him in.

"He doesn't seem to think it possible that any group of people could simply be a group who liked each other's company," an early critic of his told me. "It always has to *represent* something. And once you've determined what it represents, you look it up in a table to see if your income bracket entitles you to belong!"

Harris not only assumed that he was a close friend of every friend of Lorna's but that he had always been one, that his new "social position," as he unabashedly called it, had been retroactively conferred. He would make speeches at anniversary parties as though he had known the married couple since the wedding itself, rising to his feet with the easy assurance of a former usher or even best man and toasting the embarrassed couple with a preliminary anecdote that would have been considered rough at a stag dinner. The general exasperation, once openly acknowledged among the friends, soon rose to a fever pitch. It was decided that someone should speak to Lorna.

This was a delicate matter to bring up, and there was considerable speculation as to who had best do it. I refused myself, on the grounds that any advice about how to manage Harris had far better come from a woman, but I was in no way responsible for the disastrous choice of Lorna's mother. Mrs. Findlay regarded her daughter with a detached, not unfriendly amusement that was particularly galling to Lorna, who admired her for all the qualities that she lacked herself. Her mother at seventy was a tall, straight, self-controlled, blue-haired lady who lived in great comfort on the annuity that she had purchased with the remnant of the Findlay fortune that she had not already spent on herself. She was a supremely, almost admirably selfish woman who played bridge all night with her own snappy crowd. When I came early one evening to Lorna's for dinner I found her and Mrs. Findlay facing each other across the fireplace. Lorna looked pale and tense. I recognized the expression of wounded dignity that she had wasted on so many minor occasions. Her mother was stroking a little black poodle at her ankles.

"Well, ask Peter," Mrs. Findlay said as I came in. "If you don't believe me, ask Peter."

"No, Mother, please," Lorna said, shaking her head sharply. "Let's drop it, shall we?"

"We were discussing Mr. Grant," Mrs. Findlay said to me, disregarding her daughter's plea. "I was telling Lorna that everyone finds him too much of a cowboy. She ought to tone him down, don't you think? Take away his lasso or something?"

"Harris Grant happens to be a very important man," Lorna said with dignity. "He is not only chairman of the board of — "

"What in the world has that to do with it?" Mrs. Findlay interrupted. "He could be Julius Caesar and still improve his manners, couldn't he?" Here she turned to me. "What Lorna will not see, Peter, is that she has a responsibility to this man. She ought to be smoothing off his rough corners. What else is her background for? That's the way the English have done it for generations. It's the reason they still have a crown and a peerage today."

"You want Harris to be like the rest of you!" Lorna said with sudden heat. "You want to emasculate him, that's what you want!"

Mrs. Findlay threw up her hands.

"Did I say any such thing, Peter?" she demanded. "Did you hear me say any such thing?"

"Not while I've been here."

We couldn't, however, go on with the subject, for just at this point Harris himself walked into the room.

"Didn't hear what, Peter?" he was beginning in his jovial tone when he saw Mrs. Findlay. He stopped and reached out both arms dramatically toward her, a broad smile on his face. "Well, if it isn't my best girl!" he exclaimed. "Why didn't you tell me your mother was coming tonight, Lorna? I'd have looked forward to it all day!"

He took hold of both Mrs. Findlay's hands and shook them slowly back and forth while he stared at her with smiling eyes. I have forgotten to say that one of his worst social faults arose from his conviction that every woman over sixty liked to be flirted with the way young men in the movies sometimes flirt with their darling old grandmothers. Mrs. Findlay, unfortunately, was the last woman in the world to play this game with. She tried to free her hands with an expression of unconcealed distaste, and when he still held on she jerked them loose and examined them as if looking for marks of his violence.

"I never knew you used both hands for a greeting, Mr. Grant," she retorted. "I thought you had to keep one free for your pistol."

But he only roared with laughter.

"Oh, I was safe, Mrs. Findlay," he exclaimed. "I had hold of both of yours!"

Lorna was not her usual self for the rest of that evening.

She was bitter and angry and showed it in the sultry glances that she kept darting at her mother. She must have assumed, poor woman, with her characteristic obtuseness, that her friends and even her mother would see Harris in the same bright light in which she saw him. He was different, of course, but to her admirably different, and now she found herself in the awkward position of a child who holds up proudly to a parent a piece of tin or a battered can found in the street only to be told, in the sharpest tones, to drop it immediately, to put it down, that it's a dirty thing and might make him sick. There would never be a way for her to impress her unimpressible mother or to eradicate, lurking behind Mrs. Findlay's bland intolerance, the handsome, smiling indifference of Bill Treadway. They could always admit, her maddening parent and even more maddening ex-husband, all the wonderful qualities in all the wonderful people in the world and never feel for a moment that these things even touched on the question of their innate, accepted superiority.

"I think it's the most outrageous thing I ever heard in my life!" Lorna exploded to me at dinner when the other guests were engaged in conversing pairs. "Who do they think they are, anyway, that they have any right to criticize a man like Harris? Just because he hasn't spent his life trying to decide which of Grandpa's pictures to sell to pay the grocer! Just because he happens to have made an important contribution to our national life! And as for Mother, isn't she the limit? When you think how nice Harris has always been to her, too!"

I didn't bother to point out that she was being unfair to the friends, because it was obvious that she was in no mood to listen to reason. I was impressed with the strength of her new courage; in the past she had not been so willing to go against the feelings of her group. I assumed, and as it turned out, correctly, that she derived her new independence from a stronger hold on Harris's affections than any of us had suspected.

"They'll see," she told me darkly. "They think nobody could be happy outside of their tiny circle. That their narrow little judgments are final. I'm not so sure of that, Peter. Not the least bit sure."

She and Harris were married the following week in Foley Square by a judge. Mrs. Findlay, I found out later, had only been informed of their plans an hour before the wedding, and the rest of us learned it for the first time when we read our morning papers. It was odd, considering how long Lorna and Harris had been going about together, that we were all so surprised. It showed how little we had thought of poor Lorna's chances of catching another man.

I had rather expected, having been neutral in the Harris battle, that I might see a good deal of them when they came back to New York after a combined honeymoon and business trip of several months to the Middle East. I was surprised, therefore, that Lorna did not even call me when she returned. Apparently she was quite taken up with Harris's business world and had no intention of slipping back into the old crowd, and while I could hardly criticize her for this, it is never pleasant to feel that one is being improved on.

I decided that the first gesture, if any, would have to come from me, so I asked them to dine with me at my club. I asked them well in advance, and they accepted, and I made an effort to get together a congenial group. Two days before the party, however, Lorna called up and backed out.

"Look, Peter, dear, I know it's perfectly terrible but what can I do?" she wailed. "One of Harris's biggest stockholders is in from Nebraska with a perfectly grim wife, and I've got to throw a shindig for them and have all the oil people and Senator McKim and Lord knows who else. A ghastly bore, but you understand, dear, don't you?"

I understood. What irritated me was her assumption that I would. And even more, her assumption that I would swallow, as she evidently had swallowed, her own belief that it really *was* a bore, that she would rather be with us, the old, benighted, left-behind friends. Her resentments had quite vanished in her new superiority. Harris indeed had picked her up and carried her off. He had only visited among us long enough to find himself a wife and was now, from all we heard, moving on to newer spheres to match his constantly expanding income.

Lorna, however, had always been scrupulous about returning invitation for invitation, and a few days later I was asked to a dinner party at her large, new, conventionally modern apartment. The long white living room was full of people when I arrived, none of whom I knew, and I had to stand for several moments in front of Lorna, who was talking to Senator McKim, before she turned and greeted me.

"Darling Peter!" she exclaimed, in a voice that was

affected even for her. "What ages it's been! Senator, here's an old friend, Peter Westcott. Well, Peter, how are things? Writing like mad, I suppose?"

It was the question that expected no answer, the smile that solicited no response, the affectation of friendliness that we undertake for people whom we have not seen since our childhood and recognize with curiosity, even with amusement, but not with feeling. I had less the sense of being dropped than of being met after an interval too long to go behind.

"Have you seen Mr. Grant?" she asked. "He'll be so happy to see you."

"Mr. Grant?"

She stared.

"Why, my husband, of course!"

"I did call him Harris, you know."

But she didn't get it; she smiled at me vaguely and then turned to a new arrival. I walked across the room, feeling more puzzled than hurt, wondering if Lorna's change could possibly be genuine, if the world could really seem that different to her now. My thoughts were interrupted by the sight of Mrs. Findlay alone on the sofa. She looked more surprised than displeased at her solitude, which was evidently a novelty to her. When I came over and sat down by her she greeted me with more warmth than she would have at a party in her own milieu.

"Why, Peter!" she said. "How nice! I wouldn't have thought you were grand enough for this."

I looked around the room.

"Are we so very grand?"

She raised her eyebrows, as if shocked.

"Can't you see? All the great. The great of oil, that is. Lorna does this every night now. Surely you've heard of the Grant parties?"

I shook my head.

"But, my dear, they're famous! The dullest in New York!"

There was no spite in Mrs. Findlay's tone, not even the suggestion of a sour grape, as she said this. She was simply amused by a daughter who had fallen by the wayside of other values.

"Maybe it's necessary for Harris's business," I suggested.

She greeted this with a snort.

"You can't get her off on that, my boy," she retorted. "He was doing well enough before he married her. No, the answer is that Lorna loves it. The only thing she can talk about is how much money all these people have. She's become common, that's what happened. Cheap."

"Lorna cheap!"

"Well, wait till you talk to her."

"And we thought she was going to smooth off *his* rough edges!"

Mrs. Findlay gave a hard little laugh at this.

"She's roughened up her own, that's what she's done. She's the worse of the two. All the things I pumped into her from childhood have come out like hair rinse."

Dinner was announced. At table I was two down from Lorna and could hear everything that she said. I had to concede that what her mother had told me was true. She talked steadily about Harris and his success, about the job in Washington that he had turned down because the company had told him he was indispensable, about her house in the country and the difficulties of moving seven servants down from New York, about how she had wanted to buy a little Ford for herself but that naturally Harris had made her get a Cadillac. "When one is married to a man like Harris, after all — " she would say and then shrug her shoulders as if her audience would, of course, recognize the inevitability of her loss of freedom. It was incredible. At first I was angry, then distressed and finally amused. What, after all, was there to be angry or upset about? Lorna was happy. She would never again have to bow her head before the arrogance of her mother's or her first husband's world. Who, after all, were they to be feared by one who lived with Harris in the world of accomplishment, the world where people *did* things?

After dinner, when the ladies had left us, Harris came over and sat by me to drink his brandy. He was in a mellow mood.

"What do you think of Lorna?" he asked me, his face beaming. "Do you find her any different?"

"Well — no, not exactly."

"You don't, really? So many people tell me she's changed since we married."

"I think she's even prettier," I said hastily, "if that's what you mean."

"She is, isn't she?" He nodded with an air of general satisfaction, thinking no doubt of his brandy, his mirrored dining room, his notable guests, his wife. "You can't match what she's got, Peter. They don't make them that way any more. It's like what I told you the first time we met. About the old families. Remember?"

I nodded and drank my brandy in silence. I was thinking how neat it would have been, how like a Henry James novel, if Harris had become with marriage the suave, accomplished man of the world, if he and Lorna, in other words, had changed places, so that people who met them for the first time would have said what a pity it was that so charming a man should be tied down to the bride of his earlier and poorer days, a giddy creature whose head had obviously been turned by fame and fortune. But that would have been strictly fiction. Harris had not changed. All that had happened was that Lorna had arrayed herself in the colors of the one man who had wanted her.

THE GEMLIKE
FLAME

The Gemlike Flame

WHEN I LOOKED UP CLARENCE MCCLINTOCK THAT
summer in Venice it was partly out of curiosity and partly
out of affection. He had long ceased to be anything but a
legend to the rest of our family, the butt of mild jokes and
the object of perfunctory sympathy, a lonely, wandering,
expatriate figure, personally dignified and prematurely
bizarre, rigid in his demeanor and impossibly choosy in his
acquaintance. It was universally agreed among our aunts
and uncles that he had been an early casualty in the terrible
battle that his mother, my ex-aunt Maud, a violent, pleas-
ure-loving woman with a fortune as large as her appetites,
had waged over his custody with my sober, Presbyterian
uncle John. Yet I had remembered the Clarence of those
early years and how, for all the sobriety of demeanor that
had so amused our older relatives, there had also been a
persistent gentleness of manner that had gone hand in
hand with kindness, particularly to younger cousins.
Clarence as a boy had been scrupulously fair, invariably
just, in his personal dealings with me. The fact that I
choose such words may imply that he set himself up as a
judge, and there may have been a certain arrogance or at
least fatuity in this, but it is the impression of his integrity

and not his pretentiousness that lingers. If Clarence was magisterial to my childish eyes, he was also loyal.

When we met at the appointed café on St. Mark's Square I felt more like a nephew than a cousin. Clarence, tall and bonily thin, with small dry lips and a small hooked nose, with thin receding hair and dark, expensive clothes, did not seem a man of only thirty-seven. I did feel, however, that he was glad to see me.

"So at last one of the family comes to Europe!" he exclaimed with a small, shy yet hospitable smile of surprise. "And is writing a novel, too! Let us hope that Venice will do for your fiction what it did for Wagner's music. You're very good to look me up, Peter. No one does any more, you know. No one, that is, but Mother. She cannot, in all decency, quite neglect the sole fruit of her many unions." He smiled bleakly at this. "But give me the news," he continued in a brisker tone. "About all the good aunts and uncles and all the cousins like yourself."

News, however, was the last thing that he seemed to wish to hear. He interrupted me when I started on Aunt Clara's stroke with a sudden rush of reminiscence about the secret gift drawer that she had kept for us as children. When I tried to tell him about Uncle Warren's lawsuit, he broke in with apostrophes about the nursery rhymes which the old man used to write for us. What obviously intrigued him about me was the fact of our cousinship; it provided him with a needed link to the past which still seemed to occupy so many of his thoughts. His memory was extraordinary. It was almost as if he had spent his early years carefully collecting this series of vivid images which he somehow knew even then were to be his only companions in the self-imposed loneliness which the future held for him. My turning up after so many years must have given him a sense of reassurance, a proof of the facts on which these images were based whose very existence he may have come to doubt.

We dined together the following night and the one after. He helped to get me settled in a hotel that he recommended and which turned out to be just right for my needs. He attached himself to me with all the pertinacity of the very shy when they do not feel rebuffed, and I began, perhaps ungraciously, to see that he might become a problem. For, as far as I could make out, despite the fact that he spent every summer in Venice and had an apartment there, he not only had no friends in the city but no inclination to make any. He was too stiff and too reserved, and his Italian, although accurate, was too halting for native circles. He loved Italy and its monuments, but he would have preferred it unpopulated. Americans abroad, on the other hand, he had even less use for. He divided them into four categories, all equally detestable. There were the diplomats who alarmed him with their polish, the strident tourists who reminded him of the business world in New York that he had found too competitive, the women who had married titles whom he thought pretentious and finally the artists and writers whom he regarded with a chaste suspicion as people of unorthodox sexual appetite who had come to the sunny land of love in search of a tolerance that was not to be found in the justly censorious places of their origin. And he himself? Clarence McClintock? Why, he had simply come to Italy to admire it and be left alone. The noisiest Italians could be noisy without making

demands on him. That was their great virtue. It was as if
they had a self-assurance that his fellow Americans lacked
which enabled them to pass by the lone observer from
across the seas without the compulsion to turn and make
him part of them.

On the third night after our meeting I dined out with
Italian friends and was a bit discouraged, I confess, on
returning to my hotel, to find Clarence waiting for me in
the lobby. He seemed upset about something and wanted
to talk, so we went over to St. Mark's Square for a *cinzano*.
There he told me that he had had a letter from his mother.
She was coming to Venice at the end of the following
month to attend the fancy-dress ball at the Palazzo Lorisan.

"You mean she'll fly all the way from New York to go to
a ball?" I asked in mild surprise. "All those expensive
miles for one party?"

Clarence nodded grimly. "She's even proud of it," he
affirmed. "Mother's not afraid to face the absurdity of her
own motivations. I'll say that for her."

"But I rather admire that, don't you? I hope I have
that kind of spirit when I'm seventy."

There was a disapproving pause while Clarence sipped
his *cinzano*.

"Sixty-eight," he corrected me dryly. "You forget, Peter,"
he continued more severely, "that someone always pays for
a woman like Mother. I don't mean financially because,
obviously, my grandfather left her very well off. But
emotionally. She is quite remorseless in the pursuit of
pleasure."

"Oh, come, Clarence, I'm sure you're being hard on her,"
I protested. "How do you know she isn't really coming

over to see you?"

He smiled sourly.

"The Lorisan ball is far more important than I," he replied. "Though I won't deny," he conceded, "that seeing me may provide a subsidiary motive for her coming. She knows how I feel about Olympia Lorisan and that set of international riffraff."

"You mean she's coming here to *annoy* you? Don't you think that's going rather far?"

He shrugged his shoulders.

"Not altogether to annoy me, of course not. But it adds the icing to the cake. Oh, she's up to no good. You can be sure of that."

I had to laugh at this.

"Do you honestly think she cares that much?"

Clarence had to pause to think this over.

"We are the two most different people in the world," he said more reflectively, "and we know it. We each know in our heart that the other will never change. Yet we go on as if there was a way, or as if the other must be made to see the way even if he won't take it. In any event," he continued, changing to a brisker, more deliberate tone, as if embarrassed by his reverie, "she will not find me this time. I shall be safely in Rome while the Princess Lorisan's friends are debauching the bride of the Adriatic."

"You won't even stay to see your mother?"

"She can meet me, if she cares, in the eternal city. Will you go with me?"

I told him I had to stay in Venice and work, ball or no ball.

"I suppose you might even go to it?" he speculated.

"I might. If I'm asked."

"I see, Peter, that I must not overestimate you," he said regretfully, shaking his head. "You are essentially of that world, aren't you? Yet I wonder how any artist could really prefer to dance and drink with those shallow people than walk in Hadrian's Villa or in the moonlit Colosseum. Mind how you reject me, Peter. Haven't I told you that I burn with a 'hard, gemlike flame'?"

As a matter of fact, he had. He had told me the first night that we had dined together and in that same mocking tone. He had said that most people saw only the "brownstone front" side of his nature, the austere, stiff, conservative side, but that there was another, a truer side, a romantic, loyal, idealistic one. This was what he meant when he quoted Walter Pater, but the disdainful smile that accompanied his phrase made me wonder if any gemlike flame within him had not been smothered or at least isolated so that it burned on invisibly, a candle in a crypt.

"Well, some of us have to do more than burn for a living," I was saying, rather crudely, when looking up I saw Neddy Bane crossing the square alone.

"Why it's Neddy Bane!" I exclaimed.

Clarence looked up too, immediately alarmed at the prospect of a stranger.

"And who, pray, is Neddy Bane?"

"An old friend of mine," I said promptly, feeling for the first time that he was. "We went to school and college together. Let me ask him over, Clarence. You'll like him."

"Yes, why don't you do that?" he said in a dry, suddenly hostile tone. "But if you'll excuse me," he continued, glancing down at his watch, "I think it's time that I was on my way."

"Now, Clarence, wait. Don't be rude." I put my hand firmly on his arm. "It's not that late."

I turned and waved at Neddy, who stared for a moment and then smiled and started toward our table. It was suddenly important to me that Clarence should make this concession. The sight, as he approached us, of Neddy's friendly smile made me feel that the last three evenings had been a lifetime. It was as if I had been locked in a small dark library with the windows closed and Neddy Bane, of all unlikely people, was life beating against the panes.

"Neddy!" I called to him. "How are you, boy? Come on over and drink with us." And as he came up to the table I put my hand on Clarence's shoulder. "Do you remember my cousin, Neddy? Clarence McClintock?"

Neddy was my age, about thirty-three, but he was not as tall as Clarence or myself, and this, together with his gay sport coat and thick, brown, curly hair made him seem like a smiling and respectful boy at our table. He had large blue eyes that peered at one with a hesitant, almost timid friendliness, but when they widened with surprise, as they were apt to if one said anything in the least interesting, their blue faded almost into gray, the puffiness above his cheekbones became more evident and he seemed less boyish. He was weak, and he was supposed to be charming, but I have often wondered if his charm was not rather assumed by people who had been told that it was a quality that went with weakness. He had been a stockbroker in New York with an adequate future, married to a perfectly adequate wife, the kind of nice girl of whom it was said that she would bloom with marriage, that even her rather pinched features would separate into better proportions and glow when love had touched her. Conceivably something like this could have happened had another husband been her lot. She wanted only what so many girls wanted, a house in the suburbs in which to bring up her children and a country club whose male members were all doing as well or better than her husband. But Neddy was constitutionally unable to find content in any regular life. He could not even commute. He would get to Grand Central and drink in a bar until he had missed his train and every other reasonable one and had to spend the night with his widowed mother in the city. He was fond of rather dramatic collapses, of simply lying back and doing nothing when he felt pressure, refusing to answer questions or to give explanations, and his poor wife, lacking the maturity or the understanding to be able to cope with him, gave vent to her deep sense of injustice that he was not as other husbands and nagged him until he walked out on her and the children and fled to Europe.

It was like Neddy that he had made no arrangements for divorce or separation or for his own or anyone else's support. All this he left to his mother, who, far from rich, sent him a check when she could, at great sacrifice. He professed to be an artist, but he did condescend to take various jobs. He worked for a travel agency, for the French edition of a New York women's magazine, as secretary and guide to a Pittsburgh industrialist. Now, he told Clarence and me, his money had really given out and he was going back to New York.

"Well, it's been fun while it lasted," he said with his disarming smile, raising the drink I had ordered for him, "and I'm never one to regret things as you, Peter, ought to know. Peter has never really approved of me, Mr. Mc-Clintock," he continued turning his attention suddenly to Clarence. "Peter is the greatest bourgeois I know. Despite his writing and despite his being over here. Fundamentally, his heart has never left Wall Street."

I glanced at Clarence and noticed to my surprise that he no longer seemed bored.

"But you're quite right, Mr. Bane," he said seriously. "Peter isn't really willing to give himself to the European experience. I'm interested that you see that."

I could hardly help laughing at this unexpected alliance.

"Perhaps it's because I don't burn with a hard, gemlike flame," I retorted. "Do you, Neddy?"

Neddy glanced from me to Clarence and saw from the latter's quick flush whom my reference was aimed at.

"Do I? Of course I do!" he exclaimed. "And I'll bet your cousin here does too. Every true artist or art lover burns with a hard, gemlike flame." He turned back to Clarence. "Naturally Peter doesn't understand. What would a novelist of manners, bad manners at that, know of the true flame? I can see, Mr. McClintock, that you're a person who cuts deep into things. You have no time for surfaces. It's the only way to be. Oh, I've batted around a lot myself, as Peter here knows; I've wasted time and energy, but none of that's the real me. The real me is a painter, first and last!"

"Is it really?" Clarence asked. "But how sad then that you have to go back. People who can paint Italy should stay here. It's the only way we can contribute."

"Do you paint yourself, Mr. McClintock?"

"Alas, no. I'm a bit of a scholar, that's all. I hang my head before a real artist."

"But why!" Neddy cried. "The artist and the scholar, weren't they the team of the Renaissance?"

They continued to talk in this vein, Neddy putting himself out more and more to please Clarence. I knew his habit in the past of trying to placate the kind of disapproving figure that Clarence initially must have seemed to him at the expense of familiar and hence less awesome figures like myself. I had never, however, seen him carry it so far. When he talked about painting he deferred with humility to Clarence's amateur yet aggressively old-fashioned judgment and sought his opinion on recent exhibits. When he elicited the fact that Clarence's last monograph, on the art collection of Pius VII, was to be published in *Via Appia,* he praised the discrimination of Princess Vinitelli, its publisher. I knew that he must have heard me describe Clarence in the past as my "rich" cousin, and decided that he was simply after a loan. What really surprised me, though, was Clarence's reaction. At first he glanced at me from time to time while Neddy was talking to see if I shared his interest, but after a couple of rounds of drinks he forgot me entirely and kept his eyes riveted on Neddy. I had noticed on our previous evenings that he had drunk almost nothing, which was evidently because of a light head, for now under the influence of the mild *cinzanos* he became almost as loquacious as Neddy.

"It's wonderful to find someone who really *feels* Italy," he said, looking around at me again, but with a reproachful look. "I had begun to be afraid that the whole world was a Lorisan ball."

When I glanced at my watch and saw how late it was and got up to go, Clarence only squinted up at me, his usually sallow features softened with what struck me as an air of rather smug satisfaction, and said that he and "Neddy" would sit on a bit and have "one for the road." I left them together, amused at their congeniality, but slightly irritated at being made to feel like an elderly tutor after whose retiring hour the young wards, released, may frisk in the dark of a forbidden city. Really, I said to myself, with a sneer that surprised me, what an ass Clarence can be.

I didn't see either of them again until I ran into Neddy a week later when I was getting my mail at the American Express.

"I thought you were going home," I said.

"Well, no," he said, looking, I thought, slightly embarrassed. "I'm not exactly. Not for a while anyway."

"Where are you staying?"

He hesitated a moment and then stuck his chin forward in a sudden gesture of defiance.

"I'm staying with Clarence."

"With Clarence!" I exclaimed. "In his apartment? Why, I thought nobody ever stayed with Clarence."

"Maybe he never found anyone he wanted to ask,"

Neddy said in a superior tone.

"But how did it happen?" I asked. "How did you ever pull it off?"

Neddy was like a child in his obvious pleasure at my interest. All his pores opened happily under the reassuring sunshine of curiosity.

"Well, after you left us the other night," he said eagerly, "Clarence and I sat on and had a few more drinks. He became very reminiscent and told me about his mother and how dreadfully she had treated him when he was little. She must have been awful, don't you think, Peter? Except rather wonderful at the same time." He looked at me questioningly, afraid that his speculation was bold. I shrugged my shoulders. "Well, anyway, when I finally got up to go, just when I thought I was saying goodbye to him for good, he suddenly seized my arm and blurted out: 'If you really want to stay here and paint, you can, you know. You can set yourself up in my apartment. I'm quite alone.' Don't you think that was marvelous, Peter? From someone who looks just as cold as ice?"

"Marvelous," I agreed dryly. "And you accepted, of course?"

"I moved in the very next day! Wouldn't you have?"

"What does that matter?"

I thought over what Neddy had told me, and two days later I called on Clarence at his small, chaste, perfect apartment. He received me alone, as Neddy was out sketching. I noted that the somber living room with its carved-wood medieval statues and red damask curtains had already been turned into a studio.

"I suppose you've been wondering," he told me in his cool formal tone, "whether or not I've taken leave of my senses."

"No, Clarence. I'm just interested, that's all."

"As a cousin or as a novelist?"

"As a friend."

He looked at me suspiciously for a moment and then, nodding his head as if satisfied, proceeded in his own slow, measured pace to give me the story of what had happened. I had the feeling as he went along that his formality concealed a sort of defiance, a smug, rather cocky little satisfaction that he should have captured Neddy. It didn't matter what I thought; I was simply a person to whom an accounting had to be rendered, a visiting parent at the school where Clarence was headmaster. He admitted, to begin with, that he had been terrified at what his unprecedented impulsiveness might have led him into. Never before, he assured me, had he assumed so much responsibility for a fellow human being. But Neddy, it appeared, had soon set his mind at rest. He had proved as docile and pliable as a well-brought-up child, not only applauding the quiet and orderly routine of Clarence's life, but earnestly adapting it to his own. Clarence had found himself the preceptor of a serious and dedicated art student.

"What Neddy needs," he told me gravely, "happens to be exactly what I can offer: order and discipline. I get him up every morning at eight and send him off with his sketchbook. In the afternoons he paints in here." He pointed proudly to an easel in the corner of the living room on which stood an unfinished painting of a canal after the manner of Ziem, colorful and dull. "In the evenings we relax, but in a tempered way. We dine out in a restaurant and drink a bottle of wine. But that's all. Bed by eleven is the rule."

"I see that it's wonderful for Neddy," I said at last. "But what, Clarence, is there in it for you?"

He stared at me for a moment and then shook his head thoughtfully.

"Well, if you don't see that, Peter, what *do* you see? It's what I have always waited for."

When I walked back to my hotel I reflected with some concern on these words of his. I couldn't help feeling a certain responsibility at having been the agent who had brought him and Neddy together. Yet who was I to say that it was a bad thing? I had seen Clarence before he had met Neddy and I had seen him after, and I wondered if I could honestly say that the irritation which I felt at his blind enthusiasm for so fallible a young man was anything more than the irritation that we are apt to feel when an outsider helps one of our family for whom we have given up hope. If such was the case my doubts were the doubts of a dog in the manger.

Having established myself on a friendly basis in Clarence's new ménage, I was asked there from time to time, but by no means constantly, during the rest of the summer. It was apparent that both Clarence and Neddy were slightly on the defensive with me. The mere fact that I had previously known both of them without losing my head over either may have seemed an implied reproach to the extrava-

gance of their mutual admiration. When two weeks passed
in August without my hearing from either of them, I
assumed that Clarence had carried Neddy off to Rome to
avoid the pollution of the city by the influx of guests for
the Lorisan ball. It was with surprise, therefore, that I
received a card one morning from Aunt Maud, Clarence's
mother, telling me that she had arrived at the Grand Hotel
and asking me to come in that afternoon for a drink with
her and Clarence and "Clarence's friend."

Aunt Maud Dash, as she now called herself, having resumed her maiden name after the last of her marriages, had
done me the dubious honor of singling me out from the
other members of her first husband's family on the theory
that I was not "stuffy," or at least, as she sometimes qualified it, not quite as stuffy as the rest. There was also, of
course, the fact that I was comparatively young, male, unattached, and last but not least, a writer. When I came
into her sitting room at the hotel I found her on a chaise
lounge, her large round figure loosely covered by a blue
silk negligee, examining with a careful, almost professional
interest, a wide ruff collar that was obviously a part of her
ball costume. Her hair was pink, a different shade than
when I had last seen her, and her skin, dark and freckled,
was heavily powdered. Propped up in her seat she looked
as neat and brushed and clean as a big doll sitting in the
window of an expensive toy store. There was nothing,
however, in the least doll-like about her eyes. They were
small and black and roving; they seemed to make fun, in an
only half-goodhearted fashion, of everything about her,
even of her own weight and of the stiff little legs that stuck

out before her on the chaise longue and the wheezing, asthmatic note of her breathing.

"Why, Peter," she called to me, "you've got a corduroy coat! We'll make a bohemian out of you yet."

"Maybe it's time I went home."

She turned away now from the ruff collar and examined me more critically.

"Not yet, dear. Wait a bit. You're almost presentable now. I always said there was a chance for you."

"It's what has given me hope."

She snorted.

"Tell me about Clarence," she said abruptly. "I know I can count on you. They say he has a boyfriend."

"Neddy Bane is not exactly a boy," I replied with dignity. "He's my age. As a matter of fact I introduced them. Neddy's wife used to be a friend of mine." I hoped by this to change the direction of her thinking. It was a vain hope.

"Now look here, Peter Westcott, if you think you can put me off with some old wives' tale at my time of life and after all that I've seen — " She stopped as we heard steps in the corridor and then a light, authoritative knock on the door.

"Mother?" I heard Clarence's voice.

"Come in, darling, come in," she called, and the door opened to admit Clarence followed by a rather sheepish-looking Neddy. "How are you, my baby," she continued in a husky voice that seemed to be making fun of him. "Give your old ma a kiss."

Clarence bent down gingerly and touched his cheek to

hers, emerging from her embrace with a white powder spot on his face that he immediately, without the slightest effort at concealment, proceeded to rub off with a handkerchief.

"And is this your Mr. Bane?" Aunt Maud continued in the same voice. "What sort of man are you, Mr. Bane? Are you as severe and sober as my Clarry?"

"No, but I try," Neddy answered shyly. "Clarence is my guide and mentor."

Aunt Maud looked shrewdly from one to the other and grunted.

"Are you going to the ball, Mother," Clarence put in quickly, with a bleak glance at the ruff collar, "as the Virgin Queen?"

"Clarry, dear, your *tone,*" she reproached him. "But since you ask, child, I am. I've always liked the old girl." She turned suddenly back to Neddy. "Do you believe in the theory that she was really a man, Mr. Bane? Nobody ever saw her, you know, with her clothes off."

Neddy was fingering the red velvet hoopskirts of the costume spread out on the chair beside him.

"Oh, never!" he protested with unexpected animation. "You don't think so, do you?" Then he appealed to her suddenly, with a rather sly little smile that I had not seen before. "You mean she was really a queen?"

Aunt Maud put her head back and roared with laughter.

"But I *like* your friend, Clarry!" she exclaimed. "Can I call him Neddy? I shall anyway," she continued, turning glowingly from Clarence to his friend. "And you, Neddy, must call me Maud." She nodded in satisfaction. "Perhaps you will be my Essex? I have a man's costume, too. It's over there in that box on the chest."

Neddy glanced questioningly at Clarence and then hurried over to the box and took out the red pants and doublet. He stood before the long mirror and held them up in front of him.

"But they fit perfectly!" he exclaimed, and went back again to the box. "Oh, and just look at that sword! Gosh, Mrs. Dash, I mean Maud! Don't you love it, Clarry? Do you think we could go?" He looked anxiously at Clarence.

I didn't have to look at Clarence to know that he would resent Neddy's calling him "Clarry," aping his mother so immediately. He stood there primly, his lips twitching. like a governess who has been overruled by an indulgent parent. Then he turned on Aunt Maud.

"Why must you have an Essex?" he asked sharply. "Would you not do better to search among your own con-temporaries for a Leicester? Or even a Burleigh?"

But she simply laughed, this time a high, rather fluty laugh that was just redeemed from silliness by its mockery.

"Because I *want* an Essex!" she said defiantly. "A young attractive Essex." She winked at me. "Clarence is so absurdly conventional," she continued, more maliciously. "He thinks one should only see people one's own age. As if life were a perennial boarding school. But Neddy doesn't have to be Essex, does he, Peter? He could be one of those pretty pages whom the old queen used to favor, tweaking their ears and pinching their thighs." She threw back her head and gave herself up once more to that laugh. "Or even," she added, gasping, "stifling them half to death in her musky old bosom!"

I could see that Clarence was beside himself. I could only hope that he would not interpret her laugh as I did, as a challenge to compare the relative improprieties of Neddy as an escort for her or Neddy as a companion for him. She picked up the ruff collar now and put it almost coyly around her neck.

"Don't you think it's a good idea, Clarence?" Neddy asked hopefully. "You don't really mind, do you?"

"Mind?" Clarence snapped at him. "Why on earth should I mind? You don't expect me to decide every time you go to a party, do you?"

He got up and walked across the room to the little balcony and, going out, stood by the railing and stared down into the canal. Neddy was at first abashed by his sudden exit, but after I, at Aunt Maud's bidding, had mixed a shaker of martinis from the ample ingredients with which she always traveled, he cheered up again. In a very short time he and Aunt Maud had discovered a series of mutual acquaintances and become positively noisy. I had to leave early and went out on the balcony to say goodbye to Clarence. He was still standing there, gloomily watching the line of gondolas arriving at the hotel bringing more and more guests to the hated ball. He hardly turned when I spoke to him, but simply pointed to the scene below.

"I warned Neddy about this, but he wouldn't believe me," he said. "All hell is breaking loose here."

The very next morning he came alone to see me at my hotel. He looked tired and worn.

"I want to ask a favor of you, Peter," he said gravely.

"A favor, Clarence? How unlike you. But go ahead, I'm delighted."

"It is unlike me," he agreed, frowning. "I am not in the habit of asking favors. I am sure you will be sympathetic when I tell you that I do not find it an easy experience."

I hastened to cut short his embarrassment.

"What can I do for you, Clarence?"

"You know my mother," he began rapidly. "You understand her. She'll listen to you. You can tell her that she mustn't take Neddy to this ball."

"But why mustn't she?"

"Why?" he exclaimed in a suddenly shrill tone. "Good heavens, man, you can't have known Neddy all your life and not see what this will do to him! Just now, of all times, when he's really painting, when for once he's got parties and girls and drinking out of his mind — "

"But one ball, Clarence," I protested.

"One ball!" he almost shouted. "One marihuana! One pipe of opium!"

"But what am I going to tell your mother?"

"Tell her — " He paused and then appeared to give it up. A bitter look came over his face. "Oh, tell her," he went on harshly, "that as long as she's taken everything she could from me all my life, she may as well take Neddy too. But why she has to have her gin-soaked body hurtled in a plane three thousand miles through the ether just to interfere with the only friendship I've ever had — "

"Clarence!"

But he was completely out of control now.

"Why do I ask you, anyway?" he cried. "You like people like her, you even write about them! You think she's admirable, the old tart!"

"All right, Clarence, all right," I said firmly, putting my hands up to stop him. "I'll speak to her, I promise. But calm down, will you?"

He seized my hand in sudden embarrassed gratitude and hurried away without trusting himself to say another word. I shook my head sadly, amazed to have discovered such depths of feeling in him. I had always known that he had disliked his mother; I had not realized that he hated her. She must have seemed, in the isolation that even as a child he had preferred, the very essence of the vulgarity of living and loving as the world lived and loved, the symbol of the Indian giver, because for all her vitality he may have instinctively suspected that she wanted back the one pale spark she had emitted in bearing him. And even now, when she came to his beloved Italy, wasn't it the same thing all over again, didn't she participate more in the carnival life of the country by attending one crazy ball than he with all his monographs? That, she must have known, was his vulnerable point; that was why she struck at it year after year. It was as if she resented the very existence of what he called the gemlike flame within him and had determind to blow it out.

I telephoned Aunt Maud and invited her to have cocktails with me at Harry's Bar that afternoon. She arrived in high spirits, in a red dress and an enormous red hat, and, as I had known she would, flatly refused my request about Neddy.

"What's wrong, infant?" she asked suggestively. "Do you want to take him to the ball yourself?"

"I'm only thinking of Clarence," I retorted. "This whole

thing is bothering him terribly."

"And why should it bother Clarence?"

I noted the glitter in her eyes. It was as if she had been playing bridge with children and had suddenly picked up a slam hand, a waste, to be sure, but a hand that she could still enjoy bidding.

"You know perfectly well why, Aunt Maud," I said wearily.

"My dear Peter," she said firmly. "I know a great many things, including what stones do not bear turning over. I have no idea of asking Clarence to explain to me, his mother, what his involvement with this young man is. But I cannot see that borrowing his precious Neddy for a single evening is interfering very much. Must he have Neddy with him every second? Why doesn't he keep him in a harem?"

"You don't understand, Aunt Maud," I tried to explain. "Clarence thinks that Neddy has finally settled down to be a painter and — "

"Nonsense," she interrupted firmly. "It's selfishness, pure and simple, and you know it, Peter. Clarence is simply scared to death that Neddy will find the big world more fun than his cell. Which I should hope he would!"

"Aunt Maud," I said desperately. "*I'll* take you to the ball."

"Thank you very much, Peter, but I haven't asked you. It's all very well for Clarence to go on about my interrupting Neddy's work, but I'll bet he doesn't begrudge him the hours they waste sipping chocolate on the Piazza San Marco while he rants about his poor old mother's wicked life.

Oh, I know Clarence, Peter!"

This was a home thrust that I could not honestly deny. And what could I do, in any case, for Clarence with a mother who felt this way about him? When I wrote him that night, for I couldn't bear to face him, I made as light of it as I could. Aunt Maud, I told him, had refused to give up her "hostage."

I saw neither Clarence nor Neddy for several days, but one morning as I was picking up my mail I encountered Neddy again at the American Express. He had evidently been waiting for me for he came right over and asked if he could talk to me.

"Why not?" I said, glancing through my envelopes.

"I wonder," he began in a rather embarrassed way, "if you're not doing anything tonight, whether you wouldn't have dinner with Clarence and me. Quite frankly, I think we need a change."

"Why? Are you bored with each other?"

"It's not that exactly. But I'm worried about Clarence. He's got this fetish about my not going to that damn ball."

"Why do you go then?" I asked coldly.

"Why shouldn't I?" he protested. "Who do you think I am, I'd like to know, that Clarence can boss me around?"

"It's not a question of bossing. It's simply a question of doing a very small favor in return for the considerable number you have received."

Neddy smiled uneasily, probably the way he used to smile at his poor wife when she reproached him for spending his evenings in bars. He had almost a genius for evading any unpleasantness in the facts that surrounded him. When I failed to return his smile, however, he rather drew himself up.

"Any small financial aid that I have received from Clarence," he told me with dignity, "will be paid in full when I'm on my feet. It will not be difficult, I assure you. You probably know your cousin well enough to be aware that he doesn't play fast and loose with his money."

The impudence of this quite took me aback.

"Why do you stick around him, then?" I demanded.

"You think it's all one-sided, don't you?" he retorted. "Well, you don't know the half of it. You don't have to listen to his ravings day in and day out. And when I say ravings, I mean ravings!"

"What sort of ravings?"

Neddy proceeded to tell me. I leaned against the counter and puffed gloomily at a cigarette while he unfolded, with the relish of one unjustly accused, the whole sorry picture. For the past five days, apparently, the ball had been the sole subject of their conversation. Whether in the studio while Neddy was trying to paint or during their long dinners in little restaurants, and even on Sunday when they had been lying on the sand at the Lido, Clarence had held forth on the iniquities of Olympia Lorisan's friends and their destructive effect upon all who had any serious purpose in life. Neddy, thoroughly bored, had answered less and less, but Clarence, straining after his attention, had only become more vehement in tone and more fantastic in argument, hoping apparently by the very hyperbole in his speech to instill into his threadbare subject some dash of interest to make him listen. He had exhausted the epithets of his rather chaste vocabulary in withering descriptions of the aging guests and how they would look in their monstrous costumes. He had even tried to shame Neddy by telling him how contemptuously people spoke of impecunious young men who acted as escorts for rich old women and to alarm him by insinuating what attentions his mother, aroused by champagne and late hours, might take it into her head to expect from so junior a companion. He had cut reports out of the paper of the magnificent preparations for the party, insisting on reading them aloud with prefaces such as: "Neddy, listen to this! This really *is* the limit!" And when all else had failed, when he was desperate, he had actually resorted to the argument that the ball was a Communist plot designed to bring discredit on the idle rich of the Western world.

I listened to it with a sick feeling. I could hardly deny that the whole account, even exaggerated, had an unmistakable ring of truth. But in my sudden confrontation with the full extent of Clarence's obsession, I found myself losing my temper at its fatuously smiling cause. Neddy stood before me smugly relishing each detail of his sorry story, pleased at my obvious dismay, satisfied that I would have to concede to him now that anything Clarence might have done for him was only a token compensation for what he, the long suffering, had had to put up with.

"You're nothing but a God-damn sponge, Neddy Bane!" I exclaimed angrily. "You don't deserve to be considered anything but what you are considered!"

He turned pale.

"And what is that?"

"As Clarence's kept boyfriend!"

He stretched out an arm to me in shocked protest, he opened his mouth to remonstrate, but I turned quickly on my heel and strode away.

I was quite unable to do any writing that morning. I thought how abominably Neddy had treated his wife and children, how shamelessly he had used his old mother, and even went farther back to our school days, when he had always been careful to curry favor with the strongest clique in the class. I conjured up other and more stinging things that I could have said to him and reminded myself that I had only done my duty. But at heart, all the time, I knew perfectly well that I was only repressing my own uneasiness at what I might have done to Clarence.

Retribution did not wait long. When I walked through the hotel lobby at noon, on my way out for lunch, I saw Clarence standing at the desk talking to the clerk and then I saw the clerk nod his head and point to me. He turned around as I started over to him, and I saw that he looked pale, almost stunned. His eyes met mine and wandered off in a way that was not like him.

"He's gone," he said as I came up to him. "He's gone to Padua to paint. He said he couldn't paint with me nagging him. He said awful things to me."

"Let's go out, Clarence. Let's take a walk or have lunch or something."

He followed me obediently into the little square on which I lived.

"He said you said terrible things to him," he continued in the same dazed tone. "Terrible things, Peter."

I said nothing.

"Do you think if we both went to Padua," he asked desperately, "and if you apologized and I promised not to nag him any more, he'd come back?"

I shrugged my shoulders.

"You don't think he really might?" he insisted.

"Clarence," I said firmly, turning to him, "for God's sake, let him go. You ought to be congratulating yourself that you're rid of him. You don't know that guy, Clarence. You don't know what he's like. I'm sorry I ever brought you together."

"Sorry!" he exclaimed, coming suddenly to life again. "Sorry! When it's the one thing you've ever done for me! The one thing *anyone's* ever done for me! Don't you know what Neddy is to me, Peter?"

I looked down, embarrassed.

"Perhaps!" I muttered.

"Perhaps!" he repeated scornfully. We had stopped walking and were facing each other, Clarence again the dominant older cousin of my childhood, simply angrier, that was all. "Why you couldn't even guess! For all your reading, Peter, and for all your parade of tolerance, you're as bad as Mother. You don't want anyone to be happy unless they find their happiness in some noisy ordinary way. You tremble at the least deviation from your own mean little code or even the appearance of one. That's why you and Mother leer and sneer and pretend I do things with Neddy that Italian boys do with middle-aged male tourists for a few lira!"

"But, Clarence, I never — "

"You pretend to be on the side of the angels," he continued excitedly, "but I wonder if you're not really the worst of all bigots. It's amazing to me, Peter, that someone who even pretends to write should be so entirely incapable of visualizing the kind of pure love I feel for Neddy, a love that I've looked for all my life — ah, but what's the use?"

He broke off and left me, and I stood there thinking of the hopelessness in his face, the hopelessness of ever explaining to me that even if there *was* something on which to base his mother's leer, even if her leer was inevitably and forever tied up with every emotional state on his part, still there was a quality in his feeling that was over and above what is called sublimation, a quality that made of it something higher than — but what, I asked myself with a sudden shrug of the shoulders, echoing his thought, was the use? I hurried after him, determined that while he was desperate I would not leave him alone.

On the night of the ball Clarence and I went for a walk through the crowded streets of Venice. Olympia Lorisan had come through with an invitation at the last moment, but I did not feel I could leave him. Besides, I had no costume. In the neighborhood of the Palazzo Lorisan wine was being served to the public from huge vats, and in the little squares boys shinnied up and down the greased poles. There was dancing in the streets near the palace, both for the public and for those guests who found it more fun there; ladies in sixteenth-century costumes whirled about in the arms of Venetian boys to the hectic music of strolling players. Standing on a bridge in the area we had a view of the great baroque façade of the palace, lit up by rows of

lights attached at the floor levels. In front was a wide plat-
form, covered in red, where the guests were disembarking
from gondolas freshly painted in gold or green or yellow
and covered with wide silk canopies. Other gondolas glided
under the bridge where we were standing, and the laughter
of their masked occupants floated up to us. From one in
particular we heard a loud and familiar laugh; it came to
our ears while the gondola was still under the bridge, and
Clarence drew back quickly as it emerged, but not so
quickly that he didn't see his mother in her enormous ruff,
a small jeweled coronet perched on top of her pink hair,
gesticulating with a paste scepter to friends in other gondolas. At her feet in red tights and smiling up at her —
well, we did not need to look more closely to see who that
was. Clarence turned away from the palace, and I followed him. Obviously he did not wish to be observed,
lonely and ridiculous, watching their gaiety from the shad-
ows. We did not talk but as I walked behind him, observ-
ing the straightness of his back, the erectness of his carriage,
I had a feeling that there was a process of exorcism going
on inside him, a process that was symbolized in his very act
of walking away. If his mother liked a circus, the stiff back
of his neck seemed to be saying, if Neddy liked it, if the
Venetians liked it, if *that* was all they cared about, poor
creatures, to be distracted in a distracting world, were they
really to be blamed? Was it even reasonable of him, he
seemed to ask himself, to assume that Neddy had the
patience and devotion to tend the hard gemlike flame that
burned within? Should not the true flame-tenders, the
people like himself, enjoy in solitude the special compensa-

tions of their devotion? I realized suddenly that I had become accessory, irrelevant, and I stopped, calling after him that I was going back for another look at the ball. He barely turned his head to bid me good-night as he continued his resolute stride away from the lighted palace and the gondolas that swarmed about it like carp.